Glimpses

Short Stories

Greg Metcalf

Glimpses
© 2024 Gregory Metcalf

Cover image: Elizabeth McGurrin
Cover design: Rebekah Wetmore
Editor: Andrew Wetmore

ISBN: 978-1-998149-46-9
First edition July, 2024

Moose House Publications
2475 Perotte Road
Annapolis County, NS
B0S 1A0
moosehousepress.com
info@moosehousepress.com

Moose House Publications recognizes the support of the Province of Nova Scotia. We are pleased to work in partnership with the Department of Communities, Culture and Heritage to develop and promote our cultural resources for all Nova Scotians.

We live and work in Mi'kma'ki, the ancestral and unceded territory of the Mi'kmaw people. This territory is covered by the "Treaties of Peace and Friendship" which Mi'kmaw and Wolastoqiyik (Maliseet) people first signed with the British Crown in 1725. The treaties did not deal with surrender of lands and resources but in fact recognized Mi'kmaq and Wolastoqiyik (Maliseet) title and established the rules for what was to be an ongoing relationship between nations. We are all Treaty people.

Foreword

In January, 2020, I settled into the life of an innkeeper, moving from Vancouver to Digby, Nova Scotia. As a life-long history buff, I took interest in Nova Scotia's deep and interesting history. I came to know some wonderful, colorful characters, and learned that characters abound in these parts. Local color and a deep history tend to be the ingredients that produce interesting stories.

I learned, too, that the winters here are long, with a lot of down time for a curious mind to imagine what those stories could be. I had taken an online writing course, and, armed with a new enthusiasm, I opened my laptop and began to type.

Many locals had told me that one of the nearby cottages is haunted. No one offered a story to explain the presence of this ghost, only that it existed. I began my writing journey by imagining a story behind the local legend. The result was "Glimpses".

I enjoyed the experience and began to dig further into my imagination. The result is this unapologetically strange collection of stories about this unapologetically-characterful corner of Nova Scotia.

Greg Metcalf
June, 2024

To my dear wife, Belinda, my life companion,
who not only tolerates but supports
my obsessive need to not sit still.

These are works of fiction. The author has created the characters, conversations, interactions, and events; and any resemblance of any character to any real person is coincidental.

Glimpses

Glimpses

Have you at times woken suddenly from a vivid dream, and you feel offended, because the dream is too real and you're not ready for it to end, so you don't want to wake up, and you try to force yourself back to sleep? You grasp at the images and try to pull them back to you, but they shiver and move from your touch as if they were made of water.

Much later you can still remember some of those dream images, the more vivid ones, and long after that, maybe years perhaps, you wonder if they were the images of dreams or real memories of moments you lived.

When the summer ends, everything slows. A stillness settles and I am sure it settles on everything around, not just the cottage itself. The light becomes gradually less intense and fades earlier, and then all is engulfed in grey as the windows are covered in boarding. I know the people are all gone. I don't see them go, of course. I have no control over what I see or when.

But I know they are no longer here. No more do their sounds occasionally tringle and phuzzle through the veil. No longer do I hear snatches of voices. No longer do I feel their movements. Surprisingly, I can feel movements. Not specific ones of course, but I sense them like a dull hum shifting this way and that beyond the veil. But most of all, when the summer is ended and the stillness envelopes, there are no more moments when the veil unmists and a glimpse is offered to me.

The veil. I don't know if such a thing was ever named, or who might talk of it. So I gave it my own name, a name as seemed fit to me. I could have called it a curtain, but a curtain seemed somehow too heavy a thing, and too solid. And it is not a solid thing at all, and it does not separate me, not completely. It obscures rather. It seems to me it is soft and light and not quite solid, and hides incompletely, so it is very much like a veil.

To the extent I have any memory at all, it is but a collection of glimpses I have been allowed through the veil when a patch of it will unmist. They are random, and most are disconnected and don't stitch together to make a story. Glimpse is another name I devised, for it is all they are.

I remember the first glimpse well. I know it for a terrified scream. The scream forms around a name, which I know is my name. And the scream is from my mother. I cannot recall how she looked or what she wore, how she did her hair or even whether she was beautiful or plain. I know only three things from this glimpse. For the first thing, it was my mother who screamed. For the second, it was my name she screamed. For the third, she looked upwards as she screamed.

I no longer know my name. Strangely, though, the time my memory was lost is another memory I keep. I remember I felt a thing struggle in me and squeeze itself out of me and exit with a sensation like the sound of a pop. And then it broke into a million particles of dust that merged with nothing. And with that puff of release went the very thing that made me, me.

Mostly, the glimpses are brief, perhaps a second or two, and it is hard to tell of them in any way that makes sense. Children running into the cottage, squealing with excitement. A young man all decorous in white suit and straw boater on bended knee before a girl whose joy is such that she jumps in place. A family sitting close together, all sobbing, and an opened letter in the mother's hand.

But not all my glimpses have been brief and fractured. There have been one or two that followed a path in time. Beth and Mary were but girls blossoming to womanhood when I first heard their voices trilling through the veil. Then the veil unmisted and I stood before their bed and the veil stayed open as their bodies merged and they called each other's names and they gasped and cried and then collapsed and held each other and kissed with such a tenderness. I felt a sensation that pulled at me. And I knew this was a scene of sadness, for theirs was a love they must always hide in dark corners or stolen summer days in a far-away, isolated cottage.

There passed a few years before I saw them next. When I saw them again their girlishness was gone, their voices were soft and measured, and they moved with confidant elegance. I came upon them as they cooked together, and I saw how their hands touched as they passed things to each other, and they frequently stole glances, easily distracted from their tasks, and their smiles were the smiles that come from their eyes, not only their mouths.

Then Beth came around to Mary and took her face in her hands and kissed her deeply and whispered, "I am so happy."

And Mary whispered back, "Forever."

The last time I saw them was, I think, not long ago, and now they were shorter and rounded and their hair, once loose and carefree, was cut and blown tidy and trim. Beth still held a shade of red in her hair, though now with a gentler fire, but Mary's gold had turned to silver.

They sat upon the sofa in the front room and there were packed suitcases on the floor beside them. Beth held Mary's hand in both of her own, and one of her hands gently stroked the back of it.

Mary looked around her very slowly and deliberately. She sighed and said softly, "I shall miss it so."

She coughed a little and made to rise. Beth stood quickly and put her arm under Mary to help her. Then she called outside and a man rushed in to take their cases.

Mary walked tenderly and her lover held her close. And I knew this was a scene of pain and loss.

The man with the monocle was a writer. When I found him in a glimpse he was seated at the desk in the alcove behind the kitchen. I thought it a strange place for a visitor to sit when the sun shone so brightly outside and the veranda offered a pleasing shade. But then I saw the desk was piled high with papers and he worked furiously on one. He moved his pen across the page with great impatience and aggression. I wondered what he wrote. He paused for a moment and looked up. His eyes burned with anger and hatred. I felt a sensation that pushed me backwards, a small involuntary movement. The man's eyes instantly narrowed and focused on the spot where I stood. At that moment the veil composed its mist again and my milky view was ended.

Just as happened with Beth and Mary, I saw him again some years later. He no longer sported a monocle for effect, but wore spectacles instead, presumably for need. He no longer abused paper with a furious pen. Instead he had a typewriter, but still he hit the keys with fury.

As I stepped to the glimpse, I recognized him. I hesitated, remembering that other moment when he seemed to sense me. I watched him rattle the typewriter then hit the lever to slam the roller back to its home.

Then he stared at the paper, sighed and growled, "The end," which he followed with a cursing word I shall not repeat.

He took in a deep breath. His face composed and it was angry but it was also sardonic.

Then he reached into his drawer. He pulled out a revolver. I felt a sensation, that pushing sensation again and again his eyes moved quickly to focus on where I stood. He stared for a moment, he shook his head and his smile twitched. I believe he quietly scoffed.

Then he placed the revolver under his chin and pulled the trigger. The veil closed as his head exploded. This was a scene of betrayal, and I know not why.

There is a long absence of glimpses after that one. I think that for a long time after, no visitors came. But all things are forgotten in time, and eventually they did. The final glimpse of Beth and Mary I have already described took place long after that gunshot.

There is an empty feel to the ending of summer each year. There are occasional visitors still, I imagine people who find the fire and blaze of fall's forests is worth the chiller air and occasional rain. But eventually the last visitors leave, the cottage stills and grows endlessly quiet.

Then the veil's mist thins away and I am no longer hidden. During these months I am in the cottage itself, as if I myself am a visitor. I wander through it. I will myself to know it, even though I know my memories, if not glimpses, will always free themselves of me. I am successful I think, if only a little, for I have some impressions that remain.

The cottage is constructed from rough logs. The logs were cut and taken down as they were on the tree. They were arranged together and nailed in place with bark intact. Although I am sure some treatment was applied when first they fixed the logs, the treatment did not withstand time very well.

When summer is ended and the fall air invades the cottage, the bark on the logs cracks, it breaks into small pieces and falls. It gathers in a mess on the floor, where the dry air of winter will turn much of it to dust.

The rodents find it good supply for their nests and with the windows shuttered and the air dimmed and the scent of humans no longer a threat they will make their way in and explore at their leisure.

When first I saw them I felt discomfort and I foolishly looked for ways to avoid them. I must once have feared these creatures. Now I wait for them. As the air cools I know they will scurry to prepare their winter nests and they will come. I watch them and admire their busy behaviour and I wish I could offer them something to eat or take for their nest.

I have followed them many times, surprised at their ability to squeeze through impossible gaps and climb impossible reaches. I have tried to make noises that might attract their interest but I have no voice.

Sometimes squirrels invade and I fear for them that they might set off the traps left for the mice. Whenever those traps spring and make their kills I feel a sudden moment of wrongness and the briefest hint of a glimpse. It discomforts me, and I think if a trap were to take a squirrel it would not kill outright but the creature would suffer terribly. I do not want to know that experience.

One late fall day, not too long ago, I was surprised as a key turned in the lock and the front door opened. No one came this late in the year and I suspect the veil was ill-prepared.

I saw a man walk in as if it was normal for me to see such a thing. The man wore long boots and clothing that looked fit for working. His sleeves were long but rolled up to his elbows. On his head was a woollen cap. He carried a pencil, a small notebook and some other device I could not recognize.

He stepped inside and stood for a moment, glancing around the dim interior. He tugged at the small device as a distraction, pulling something out and letting it snap back in. In and out, in and out. I recognized the markings of a measuring tape.

He left the door open and I did not like this. It made me vulner-able with no veil around me, so I caused it to shut. I do not know how. I needed it shut and it was.

The door closed firmly, not with a bang but firmly enough that the man turned with alarm. He studied the door with a frown.

Then he looked around again, peering intently.

I stepped back into a corner where the shadow was deep and I thought of the veil and how it is another thing I do not control.

"Go away!" he called. "Leave me."

I froze in place. I tried to think of what I might do next, but no idea presented itself.

But the man was more anxious than I. Whatever he had come to do, he changed his mind. After another quick look around, he left and locked the door behind him.

He returned later that day, with another man. This time when he opened the door he closed it gently behind him, I thought it re-spectful the way he did that.

He had in his hand another instrument that shone a bright light and he flicked it around to light up every corner in turn. This time I observed from the upstairs balcony that fronted the bedrooms. I did not like it much up there, but nonetheless I stayed very still.

The second man seemed to be amused and teased the first man, but not too badly, for I think he was subordinate to the first.

At last the first one seemed satisfied. They took out their other devices and proceeded to take measures, which they wrote into their notebook. They discussed ideas that suggested they would be making alterations or repairs.

And so it was that a team of them arrived a few days later and I heard the sounds of materials unloading and instructions being called, but by then the veil had re-formed and I only felt the sounds and motions of their team at work.

My time drifts between the busy summers and the quiet fall and winters. I have wondered at times if the presence of people in the summer gives me comfort. Each year I have tried to examine my off-season existence to see if it differs. Am I lonely? Am I bored? But how would I know? I do not determine my memories, so I have no idea what lies between them. All I can say is that I pass through the summer months and arrive at fall, and I pass through the fall and winter months and arrive at spring and summer and I pass through again.

And then comes today. This very morning. I am beside the window in the kitchen. It is shuttered, but the shutters are ill-fitted and there is a gap. It is my favourite place to stand. I am able to look through the gap and it looks upon the path that winds through the forest.

Fall is past and the trees have shed their robes of red and gold. All the trees are grey with naked branches that reach and stretch like deformed fingers pleading for sun. A light snow lies on the path and dusts the trees here and there.

I think it a pretty scene. I think I may stay awhile, perhaps all day until the darkness settles in the late afternoon. I may see a deer or two and they will pause and turn their heads and raise their ears as they fear being watched, which they are, but know not.

Then I hear a voice. The voice of a man. He calls a name. "Annie!" The voice is strained, it wants to be loud but cannot.

I move aside so I can peer through the gap at an angle. I see a trail of shuffling footsteps that have turned into the cottage garden towards the front door. I see a fraction of a coat and a booted foot. But no more.

I wait. The man will leave shortly.

But he calls again. "Annie. I know you are there, Annie."

Who is Annie? Why does he call her? The cottage attracts many visitors and I have known the names of only a few, so it is not surprising if I do not know her. But why does this man think she is here?

I do nothing, for nothing is to be done.

I hear footsteps outside, but they do not head back to the path. Instead they track around the side of the cottage, then they climb the short steps onto the veranda and I hear them clump, clump on the wooden deck.

"Annie," he calls again.

He tries the back door that leads to the veranda, but it is also locked. He steps off the veranda and around the other side, to the small door at the back of the kitchen. It too is locked, but the door is loosely fit and quite flimsy. I can see it move as he tries it. I hear the man breathing deeply. I believe his efforts have tired him.

There is a moment when I think he may have left. Then I hear a loud bang and the kitchen door moves violently. This is followed by another bang and the door crashes open.

The man stands in the doorway with a large stone in his hand. He drops it and takes deep, ragged breaths. I see him in silhouette, for the light behind him frames him in the doorway. He is small and stooped.

He comes inside with fragile steps, his hand reaching to the kitchen counter for support. He is an old man. He struggles for a moment then he draws a deep breath to fill his lungs and settle his breathing.

He looks up. He looks at me!

"Hello Annie," he says, and I am assailed by sensations that fly through me and around me and take me off balance and I am buffeted backwards, and I gasp and I did not know I could gasp, and I cry out and I did not know I could cry out.

He reaches out to me, as if to take my hand. "Annie," he says again.

Will he stop using that name? I feel a pain when he says it like a whip has been cracked against my skin and I do not know if the name causes the pain, or the voice that calls the name.

I back away and I put up my own hand and I do not know if I mean to stop him or stop the images, for I am suddenly assailed by images from a dream that I left unfinished so very long ago.

I am newly fifteen, and my dress is a gift from my parents. I am pretty in my dress of pastel pink. I know this for everyone tells me how pretty I am, and I am happy with their compliments but I search only for his face.

"Jared!" I call out.

I did not know I have a voice. It is dry and powdered like stiffened hay. I stare at him and I know my eyes are wide.

He nods stiffly and takes another step towards me.

I step back again, urgently. How does he see me? How does he talk to me?

He makes as if to move again, and I step back wildly. "No!" I croak.

"Okay, okay. I will stop. I will go no further." He leans back so he can rest against the kitchen counter. He is feeble, but I feel something unpleasant radiating from him and I am filled with discomfort.

The pink dress. I am wearing it. I see it. How do I see it? I see my arms, I touch my hands to my face and I feel it. I am afraid and I did not know I could be afraid.

The images flash in my head again. They distract me and confuse me. The pink dress. It is so pretty. It makes me so pretty. He says that. He says I am the prettiest girl in all Smiths Cove, he'd like to kiss me and I hold my face to hide my blushes and he laughs and pulls my hands away.

I look at him now, this feeble man who sees me and hears me and I am becoming whole and I do not know why and I ask him, "Why are you here?"

"I'm dying, Annie. My body is eating itself away." He takes deep breaths. In just the short time he is here he seems to weaken rapidly. "I need to..."

He coughs, and it becomes a series of coughs and he pauses to clear his throat and steady his breath.

In that pause I am assailed again. He kisses me and I am flushed and shy. I giggle because I am not sure what else to do. Then he kisses me again and he makes the kiss linger, and I feel his tongue and I am suddenly flustered and I pull away, but his mouth follows mine. I am sitting on the carpet but I fall over as he leans on me, and he climbs onto me and I feel his weight on me and I don't want that. I am not giggling anymore, I am calling his name, "Jared, Jared," and I beg him to stop.

He takes another small step forward and I put up my arms to make him stop.

"Annie, please." He lifts his hands in a pleading gesture. "I will keep a distance, but may I move to the living room to sit?"

I say nothing, but I retreat to a corner of the room to allow him space to move. He does so slowly, I can see that every step is an effort. He must have struggled walking down Harbour View Road to reach me.

He makes his way to the large wing back armchair that Daddy loved so. How do I know that? He falls into it. He closes his eyes and I think he sleeps.

I wait for a time then I move from the corner into which I have confined myself. I move to the master bedroom, where a long mirror stands in the corner and a faint spray of light presses through the crooked shuttering.

I stand in front of the mirror and I see a girl who is Annie. I have arms and I have legs that protrude daringly from below the billowing flare of the pastel pink skirt. I am whole.

Am I pretty?

But I cannot see my face. I try, but I cannot look upon it.

He does not stop. I cry out louder. He mumbles in my ear, "Annie, you are so lovely. Annie, I want you so much."

I try to push him away but he is heavy and he is strong.

"Don't you love me Annie? If you love me you'll let me," he whispers from deep in his throat, and I am bewildered.

I don't understand. I'm scared and I feel something terrible will happen, and I'm afraid he will think I don't love him and I love Mommy and I love Daddy and I love Becca, though I tease her so, and I like Jared and I want his eyes to see me but I don't love Jared and why would he think that, but if I don't love him will he be hurt and will he hate me and am I a bad person?

I move downstairs again. I stand in the middle of the living room floor.

He is recovering. His breathing is slowed and his eyes are open. I glare at him.

His hand has grasped at my breast, squeezing crudely and roughly, then he has pulled at the hem of my pastel pink skirt and lifted it. I push at him and I beg him to stop and he whispers things about love and boys and girls and love again and I feel my underwear pulled and I am entered and I scream this is wrong this is wrong this is so very wrong.

"Why are you here?" I rasp.

"We never came back here, me and my family," he says, his head moving to take in the surroundings once so familiar to him, "after what happened."

I feel something sharp and bitter moving through my body, scratching at my innards.

He continues, "I told my parents the memories were too sad. They believed me. I ran away, and I kept running. I moved from place to place, always further away from Nova Scotia. I live in California now. I studied and became a psychologist."

I frown and he says, "A doctor who treats illnesses of the mind and"—he touches his heart—"emotions. I thought I could find a way to fix what was inside me, but I could not.

"I tried to kill myself, more than once. But I lacked the courage."

I feel a wrench in me as he says this but the wrench is not for him.

I kneel in the bathtub. The pink dress lies on the bathroom floor. I try to turn the taps to run faster but they are already at their maximum. I soak a cloth and rub myself. I rub every inch of skin I can reach. I make the water as hot as I can bear it. I rub again. I lather the cloth thick with soap and I rub again. I cannot clean myself. I try and try but the stain is inside me and I cannot get it off.

"Why are you here?" I demand again.

"Not long ago a cousin came to visit. She told me the old cottage was still standing. I tried to ignore her. It's a subject I try to avoid. But she has always been one for one-sided conversations and would not be put off. She told me gossip about the families who still own the cottages in Harbourview, and then said there is a rumour that this cottage is haunted by a young girl. My cousin thought that was amusing, but as she said it, I felt a weight crush me."

He lifts his head, for he had been looking at his hands as he spoke.

"You want me to forgive you?" I am becoming accustomed to using my voice, and I ask him this in a tone of contempt.

He shakes his head. "No," he says, "god, no. I ask no forgiveness. I am here to set you free."

I have no response to this.

"When I studied psychology, I befriended a man who was obsessed with the idea of ghosts. He believed they existed, which earned him ridicule amongst a community that wanted to be guided only by science and rationality. I believed he must have suffered some personal loss that made him cling to such beliefs, but I saw no reason to spoil our friendship by suggesting it to him. Instead, I allowed him to talk of it freely and used his ramblings as interesting research in my field of studies.

"Once I asked him the question that seemed most obvious to me.

Do all people become ghosts? He assured me most vociferously they did not. Then, I wished to know, why some and not others?"

He pauses again to take in some air. I have edged forward so I am no longer completely in the shadow. I will move no closer, though, for his aura still repels me.

"My friend told me that a ghost exists for a life taken wrong." He pauses, and repeats, "A ghost exists for a life taken wrong. I wasn't sure what he meant but I thought of you when he said it, and I wondered even then if you had departed or stayed."

I cannot make myself clean. I cannot be clean again. I dry myself, roughly. I see my reflection in the mirror and I am afire with red patches where I have rubbed and dried. The pink dress lies on the floor and I step away from it. It makes me want to vomit.

But they will expect the dress and if I don't wear it they will ask why and I'm afraid what I will say, so I lift the dress and I slip it over my head. I look in the mirror and the dress hangs badly on me and it is ugly and stained with a patch of blood and I try to clean it but it will not clean and I have not put on underwear and the stained cloth touches me all over and stains me more.

"He told me that a ghost is locked in an eternal quest to feel, for the manner of their separation from life left feelings ripped open and exposed."

I think of the glimpses. The squealing excitement of young children, the climax of passion, the moment of love committed, a deep and violent anger and the ultimate despair.

"I found my old friend two weeks ago. It is surprisingly easy to find a long-lost acquaintance these days. I phoned him and spoke to a woman who said she was his daughter, but when she put the phone to his ear he was confused and incoherent. His mind is no longer whole.

"You see, I needed to ask him a question, and since he could not help me, I have worried myself with the question until the answer came to me."

They cannot see me in the dress. It is a thing of shame and I am a thing of shame. Admire me, tell me I'm pretty, make excuses so we can be alone, take my hand, kiss my lips. I cannot look at me anymore, I see stain and shame. Mommy and Daddy will see stain and shame. They cannot see me.

He reaches into his pocket and extracts a rope. "Will you help me?" He holds the rope out.

It is a real rope. A real thing, but I reach out and my hand closes around it and it is solid in my solid hand.

"You know where," he says. "I am sorry to ask but I will need your help. The stairs may be too much for me."

I cannot touch him, but I am able to hold the rope.

He holds one end and I go to the top of the stairs and I take his weight with the rope as he climbs each step with difficulty. It takes a long time, but eventually he reaches the balcony that fronts the bedroom doors. He pants loudly and roughly. His hand holds the railing to steady himself.

He lets go of the rope and with a movement of his head indicates that I know where to take it.

I walk around to the side of the balcony I always avoid. I loop the rope around the third upright from the end, the upright that always seemed the thickest and strongest. I tie a loop in the other end.

He has made his way to me as I have been busy and he stands now beside me. I feel the tightening inside me and my body heaves as if I would vomit but I only cough dry air.

I hand him the loop.

He nods and I move away, I move back down into the living room where I turn to see him using the last of his strength to climb over the railing, loop around his neck.

Then he drops.

I am whole again, for a fraction of a moment I am whole again and the dress is a beautiful pastel pink and it is pretty and I am pretty.

And then I feel a sensation like the sound of a pop and I am broken into a million particles of dust that merge with nothing.

Forever mine

I can't breathe.

I've never had to think about how to do that until now. D*raw in air, exhale.* But as I draw in, something catches and I can't help but cough, and when I exhale, the breath rushes out with a shudder I cannot control.

I have images flashing through my head. They leap from yesterday to today, from the afternoon to the night to the morning, and it would help if I could sort them or see them as they occurred, but my brain won't settle and they come at me randomly.

I can't breathe.

I am empty. Yesterday I was joy. I was filled. I floated. But I am empty now.

> It is yesterday morning on Water Street. I am basking in the sun and giggling and not minding the looks I attract from people dressed in their best strolling outfits. It is a lovely day and it will be lovelier still.

It is this morning and I hide in the ticket office of Digby Station and watch from the small window as the train departs. I am well concealed.

The ticket officer looks at me strangely as I peer out of the window, and tells me I am free to go onto the platform. But I shake my head and stay in hiding.

> The afternoon was our afternoon. We had planned it for weeks.

He had promised to join his friends for a departing drink in the evening. I wished it were not so, but I was happy that the afternoon was just for us.

The train whistles and I think it whistles for me, mocking me. "Fooooooooool" it blows. "Fooooooooool," again.

All those boys in their smart green uniforms pull themselves away from their girls and their families and joke with each other at the fuss their loved ones make.

"Fooooooooool," the whistle blows again, and the boys hurry onto the train.

I know them, boys from school, boys who flip burgers in the take-outs, boys who work the fishing boats in the foulest of weather.

"Fooooooooool," one last time.

He borrowed his dad's Dodge and he felt so proud because his dad had never let him borrow it before. We drove it to Smiths Cove, where he had booked us a room at the Harbourview Inn.

The inn was grand. The lobby was surrounded by gleaming, polished wood and the carpet was thick and soft underfoot. I wanted to take off my shoes and walk on it barefoot, but I thought they would mark me as simple if I did that.

There was a gramophone in the corner, set in a cabinet made of polished maple. It played what played everywhere, but here Vera sounded less commonplace and therefore more touching.

> We'll meet again,
> Don't know where, don't know when.
> But I know we'll meet again some sunny day....

And I looked at him and squeezed his arm and rested my head on his arm to be demure, but also to hide the tears that welled.

When we came to the check-in desk, the wife glared at us and asked if we were married, but her husband laid his hand on her arm and squeezed. He took our payment and passed us the key with a smile. I smiled back at him and mouthed a thank you.

As we walked away to our room I heard the husband whisper, "He's shipping out tomorrow. Give them a break."

The boys in smart green pull away from their loved ones and head to the train, but my eyes fix on just one. He turns this way and that, he makes to turn for the train, then he looks around again and his face is frowning and, though I am a distance away, I see him wipe away a tear.

Then his friends call him and he finally backs towards the train, still searching, until he stands on the steps and closes the door.

He strains out of the window and looks backwards as the train pulls away and it calls out again, "fooooooool."

We had both emptied our savings to be sure we could be in a special place for our special time, and the room at Harbourview Inn was magical. It was bathed in the afternoon sun and everything seemed washed in a filter of soft gold.

I didn't know a bed could be so big and so high off the floor. Its spread was embroidered with delicate flowers like I imagined the finery of a royal chamber.

There were two comfortable armchairs tucked in the corners, and the carpet was as soft and inviting as the one in the lobby.

We giggled and jumped on the mattress and it was impossibly soft and I thought it might swallow me, but instead it held me just like a nymph in the palm of a god. We bounced on it like little children, giggling until we tired and lay ourselves flat, side by side.

The night was to be his night with his friends, a promise he'd made to them.

I didn't like it when he told me. I wanted all his time before shipping. But he smiled at me and kissed me on my forehead and said I was so adorable when I was jealous, and I couldn't help but smile back, and I playfully smacked him on his chest, and he hugged me and whispered, "After our afternoon together you'll be wanting to sleep anyway."

And I giggled and blushed and he laughed some more.

I watch the train shrink into the distance.

The ticket officer asks me if I am okay and I nod, but his face says he knows I am not. He comes around the desk and offers me a handkerchief and I think of all the films where the heroine cries and the hero offers her a handkerchief, and I think I am a wretched sort of heroine.

I thought I would struggle against being naked with him, I thought my nerves would overcome me and make me shy and simple and I'd surely disappoint him.

But as we lay on the bed after our playful bouncing, we looked at each other with a tenderness that made my insides tighten exquisitely, and I knew the moment was right for us, and suddenly my hesitation vanished.

I kissed him and I began to unbutton my blouse. He stopped me and asked me if I was sure, and I kissed him and told him I was never so sure. I was full of desire for him, and I felt a confidence I never suspected was in me.

My desire and assurance surprised me. It was beautiful and primitive and it delighted me.

But I had not thought of him.

He struggled to respond to me. I had been too eager and I must have overwhelmed him.

He asked me to stroke him with my hand while he lay on his back with his eyes closed, and when I leaned to whisper in his ear he shushed me and used his own hand to show me what to do.

After a few minutes he hardened, and when he did, he quickly turned me over and entered me.

He moved in me rapidly. In a few seconds I felt him shudder and it was done.

He seemed on the verge of sobbing and he spoke in a broken voice. He was sorry, but his mind was filled with everything to come, and could I forgive him and wait for a time when his only thoughts were of me?

I felt so badly for him and I held him tightly.

We lay together all afternoon, our bodies wrapped together. We talked about the end of the war and our lives together and we made a future story for ourselves that was perfect in every way, and I told him our lovemaking would wait and would be something wonderful for us both.

The night was his to spend with his friends, and when we returned to Digby and parked the Dodge, we parted and I wanted to cry. We kissed and he held me and he whispered to me that he loved me, really, and asked me to believe him, and of course I did and told him so.

Then he smiled and turned to walk away, but first he reminded me not to be late in the morning, as the station might be thronging with people, and I giggled and told him I'd probably be there hours before departure so I could watch him arriving in his smart new uniform.

Then he was gone and I was left to my own thoughts.

I tried to relax at home. My dad had the radio tuned to the

news.

Hearing about the war only made me anxious. Everything sounded more positive now, after the early years of setback and defeat. But as the allies advanced it seemed Canadian forces were closer to the main fighting, and when I heard the names of the far away places in Africa and Italy, my mind tricked me with images of him rushing into a hail of bullets.

When the broadcaster talked about the bravery of our Canadian boys I couldn't take it any more and I went to my room. But I only thought of his torment that afternoon and how it couldn't be right for him to cross the ocean with a worry like that in his head.

When the train has left, the station empties quickly. Then I leave the ticket office and walk onto the platform. There is no whistle now, and the station has grown strangely quiet.

I don't know what to do. Should I go home? At home I would go to my room and think, and I didn't want to think. I can't go to work as I don't have a shift.

I'd expected that when the train left I'd meet some of the other girls and we would console each other, but they are gone and I am alone.

In my bedroom I tried to read a book but the words blurred. I worried myself with images of him trying to be brave in a field full of bloody bodies and foul odours, and I tried to fill my head with memories of our special afternoon.

I needed one more moment alone with him so I could tell him that I understood, and reassure him that our afternoon was special anyway, and that I loved him, really, and he should not worry about us, and I could beg him to keep his head down and make him promise me not to be brave. I couldn't sleep until I'd held him just once more.

So I slipped on my coat and told my parents I needed air. Bless them, they didn't protest.

I knew they'd be at the pub near the wharf, and it was only a walk of thirty minutes before I was standing outside.

I didn't want to be conspicuous and embarrass him in front of his friends, so I walked down to the waterfront and sat on one of the benches, where I could see up the lane leading to the pub entrance. I knew he'd be longing to see me again even after a few drinks, just as I longed to see him. I'd wait until he and his friends parted ways, and then I'd surprise him.

I stand on the empty platform and the silence hits me. The train is long gone, and him with it. To Halifax it is bound and there they will board ship right away. There is no stopping until they've crossed the Atlantic and reached their training base in England. How long before they board ship again and sail to Italy or North Africa? I tremble, and my head spins.

I waited for half an hour before a shaft of light flooded the entrance to the pub, and a group of shadows fell into it. I stood and moved closer, straining to see if it was them.

There was laughter and his voice was clear among it.

I smiled but I kept a distance, as I didn't want his friends to tease him that his girl is clingy.

They walked down Queen Street, and I followed. Soon, one of the friends parted. They all hugged and slapped each other's backs and said their goodbyes too loudly, with parting insults, in the way men do when they should say, 'take care.'

The rest continued walking. Another parted and another, until it was just him and one of his friends, with me following at a distance.

They walked in silence, as if each was consumed by his own

thoughts.

The platform is the cruellest place. I stand in a great empty space with nothing but echoes flowing in and out of my head.
It is warm, but the platform feels cold and I have chilling stabs all over my body, till I bend over double and cry.

He is gone and he is gone with that look of bewildered hurt etched in his face, and the cruel etching was mine.

> He neared his home and I hoped his friend would depart soon as I wanted to catch him before he entered the house. But at his house they both walked into the driveway.
>
> They didn't walk to the front door, which surprised me. Instead, they moved around the house to the small garden in the back. They stopped where there were no windows to cast a light. They were out of sight to anyone on the road, but I could see them from where I stood behind a wall a little way back.
>
> They looked around as if to confirm they were alone. Then they kissed.

I fall to my knees on the platform, and I sob. Out of the corner of my eye I see the ticket officer making his way to me, but I raise my hand and gesture him to go away.

My sobbing stretches into a loud wail that tears at my throat.

I see his face, his beautiful face knotted with hurt and bewilderment, and I hear his voice whispering to me so gently, "I really do love you, really."

> They kissed. He and another man. They kissed, and it was a deep and passionate kiss. I held my fist to my mouth to stifle a scream.
>
> I tried to process this thing but I hadn't the understanding in

my head to do so. I had heard taunts about boys who did things with other boys, but I thought those were nonsense stories invented by cruel boys to hurt boys with softer souls. I heard my father's voice laughing at a joke about fairy boys, and I saw my mother's lips purse disapprovingly that such a subject could be heard in our home.

I thought of the kisses we had shared together and my body convulsed to think of those lips touching the lips of another man. I felt vomit rise and I covered my mouth and swallowed it back. My eyes burned and I futilely wiped my cheeks.

I wanted to cry out, then I felt anger grow in my belly and rise in me until my head ached from the pressure of it.

I felt sick from humiliation, I was a fool. How could I not have known? My love, my lover, who had entered my naked body that very afternoon, who had said he loved me, really.

I turned and walked away. I walked until I was out of sight and sound and then I ran. I ran with the tears nearly blinding me and I fell more than once before I reached home.

I fell asleep, but only after hours of tormenting myself with the images I could not shake.

Eventually exhaustion overcame my body.

I woke as soon as the sun glanced past the edges of my curtain. Immediately that kiss ripped into my thoughts.

I wished it were a dream, but it was not. I knew I could not face him now. How could I look at his face when all I wanted was to tear at it and rip his lips off of it?

But I could not stay away. I needed to be there, to see him go. To be sure he was gone and the hurt was taken away from me.

Draw in a breath and let out a breath. But as I draw in something catches and I can't help but cough. And when I let go my breath it shudders and rushes out as if I have no control over it.

Those flashes in my head jump between yesterday and today, between the afternoon and the night and the morning and I can't order them as they should be. They flash like I imagine the great cannons across the ocean flash, and I feel stings of pain and I think of a hail of bullets, and my breath is beyond my control.

What have I done?

That hurt and bewildered face will find its way to a muddy field somewhere and stare down the barrels of a thousand guns, hurt and bewildered.

"I really do love you, really."

Suddenly I know. He is but a boy of a softer soul who must hide in a shadow, for he is surrounded by those of cruel hearts like me, and I hear the faint sound of the train's whistle far in the distance and it taunts me still.

"Foooooooool," it calls.

Little Pete

I once heard a sleepy town described to me like this: Saturday evenings are the highlight of the social calendar, when all the townsfolk gather with deckchairs and cooler boxes at the town centre's main intersection, where together they will spend the night watching the traffic lights change.

Smiths Cove is not like this. It lacks a centre, intersection and traffic lights. No gatherings take place. Saturday evenings are as quiet as any other. Thus, the sound of a speeding car's engine is a rather brutal interruption, sufficient to turn most heads.

I was walking Miss on Highway 1. Highway 1 is a very ordinary rural road. How it came to be named a highway has been a puzzle to me since I first moved to Smiths Cove, but not a puzzle I have been inclined to investigate deeply. It is what it is, and a popular stretch for dog walkers like me.

Some think Nova Scotia suffers dreadful winters, but that's not true. Winters are generally mild, frequently offering days when the sky proudly displays a bright, crisp cerulean hue that reflects brightly on the surface of the snow. The air has a chilled purity that is delightfully invigorating. The snow is rarely too deep for walking, while the scarcity of rain and traffic spares us from sludge.

It was the late afternoon on one of those days. Missy and I had enjoyed a forty-five minute stroll that I diligently counted as my ten thousand steps for the day. My thoughts were turning to home, a log fire, some wine and Netflix.

The engine roar came from the direction of Highway One heading towards Bear River. I looked in that direction and saw Little Pete and his dog Nobby walking towards us.

I didn't call him Little Pete to his face. Just Pete. I attached the little when I first met him, shortly after moving here. I had read something about using associations to prompt recall of strangers' names, and I had thought it a clever tactic, being a newcomer to town.

The problem is that those associations tend to stick in my brain, and I am forever worried I might blurt out something stupid like, "Hey, Little Pete, how are you today?"

Pete was, well, a little man. His cockney accent was out of place in rural Nova Scotia. He told me he had retired here to seek some peace and quiet after serving in the British armed forces and the British police.

Given his diminutive stature, I had taken that with a pinch of salt.

Nobby was also a name I had invented. I never did know that dog's real name. But he reminded me of an English soccer player called Nobby Stiles, a small, tough and aggressive player whose main job on the pitch was to swiftly nobble any opposition player possessing the ball. Hence the name.

As for Pete's Nobby, I pictured a toy pom in a close relationship with a sausage dog, and one wild night they had shared a threesome with an Arctic fox. Its face was a mystery. The very tip of a black nose was visible, and in good light it was just possible to see a glimpse of black eyes hiding behind a mane of wiry white fur.

Despite its cuddly appearance, like its soccer-playing namesake this Nobby possessed a fearsome attitude and needed no excuse to let loose an irritating cacophony of tiny snarls and yaps.

My Miss is not good with other dogs generally, and has a particular dislike of high-pitched yappers. So Little Pete and I had an understanding that, if we met and chatted, we did so from opposite sides of the road, keeping our dogs firmly leashed.

I waved at Little Pete. He waved back and turned towards the source of the noise. Then he turned back, caught my eye and shrugged. I shrugged back. Eloquence.

To the other side of me, coming out of Harbour View Road, were Charles and Camilla and their dog. Again, the name association thing. I have spoken to them once or twice, but we never exchanged names and now I am too embarrassed to ask. I named them Charles and Camilla because they are of a similar age and favour clothing in the style of English country gentlefolk. I waved to them and they waved back.

Their dog is a golden retriever. Aging and mellow, he is never disturbed by anything. Miss, however, is Miss and has no love for mellow yellow dogs, so I have a similar greeting-across-the-road arrangement with Charles and Camilla.

They also had paused their walk and stood peering to the east to see who could be approaching Smiths Cove with such urgency.

Next, Dave Yellow Jacket caught my eye. Dave is an earnest chap. Last summer I saw him plant himself in the middle of Harbour View Road, forcing an oncoming car to stop, then lecture the driver that there are often children in the area and he must be doing at least forty kilometres an hour and he should take it easy, *Buddy*.

Dave it was who once shook his head and shamed a man into scurrying back and picking up his dog's poo. Dave it was who would wear a shiny yellow safety jacket for walking, even though rush hour in Smiths Cove would barely trouble a sloth.

Dave and I are fine with each other. Both our dogs are excitable, so we avoid trouble by ensuring that when we meet we keep to, well, I think it's a bit obvious by now.

A black car came swiftly over the slight rise and raced past Little Pete, who had stepped well into the grass verge, tugging a snarling and yapping Nobby.

Pete glared at the car and I expected him to raise a fist and shout something. But he just shook his head in disgust, tugged at Nobby's lead and disappeared from site.

The black car came to a sudden stop at the church. I remembered my first trip to Smiths Cove, when the GPS had guided me to the town centre. That turned out to be the church. So, using my powers of deduction, I concluded that the driver of the car had been seeking the town centre of Smiths Cove.

The car was a BMW, most definitely not of these parts.

While Charles, Camilla, and I stood gazing, Dave puffed himself up and strode forward to confront the driver. I felt a little guilty. I was closer to the car than Dave, and it crossed my mind for a moment that perhaps I should be the one to confront.

But Dave crossed over the road quickly. I then did the appropriate thing and followed him, maintaining a prudent gap, as both Dave and I were struggling now with leashes pulled tight.

Charles and Camilla tagged along, but keeping to the other side of the road, their curiosity kept in check by the charged canine atmosphere.

As Dave neared the car he suddenly stopped.

Two figures had emerged from the car. They were both fully clothed in black. On his head, a black cloth flat cap; on hers, a loose, black crocheted hat. Sunglasses, masks, long woollen coats, shirts. All black. Even the shirt he wore beneath his coat was black. He also wore a neatly knotted tie, black. Well, grayish charcoal perhaps. A novelty sight in these parts.

They both wore trousers. Not denim, I might add. Proper black trousers. Shoes, smart and well polished. They appeared every inch to be a pair of mafia hitmen. Or should I say hit man and woman; hit persons, perhaps.

Only two details jarred. The caps and glasses could not fully disguise the lines etched deeply into their faces, nor hide the tufts of grey hair.

They looked around our little circle. The woman coughed lightly, in the way formal people do when they wish to begin a conversation. She tilted her head down and looked at us over her sunglasses.

I have never understood this habit. How is it more comfortable to contort the neck in an unnatural tilt rather than to simply remove the sunglasses when addressing someone? In any case, she looked around us.

I realized Charles and Camilla had been moved by curiosity to venture to our side of the road. We made a semi-circle, with just enough distance to keep our agitated dogs tidy.

"Good afternoon," she said, rather obviously.

Each of us mumbled, "Afternoon," and nodded, as if agreement was required on the subject of it being afternoon. The man with her nodded too, so we were evidently off to a good start.

"We've driven from Halifax," the lady stated in an accent more Windsor, England than Halifax, Nova Scotia. Her tone implied their journey was noteworthy.

I looked across at Dave and raised an eyebrow. He widened his eyes a little and gave a quick shrug. Evidently these people were a little beyond his grasp; his enthusiasm to put them in order seemed diminished.

With Dave seemingly tongue-tied, I felt a tug of responsibility. "Um," I said, "good afternoon." I fixed a pleasant and hopefully non-confrontational smile on my face. "We couldn't help noticing you seemed to be driving rather fast."

Dave nodded eagerly. Charles and Camilla moved their heads gravely.

The man shrugged and looked over at the woman, who was standing on the driver's side of the car. She shrugged back at him.

The man said, "Hmph." The woman said nothing.

I looked at Dave and Charles but found no help there. I decided the point had been made and did what seemed most appropriate. I shrugged.

Our concentration had slipped and our dogs sensed an opening. It started, oddly enough, with the mellow yellow chap snarling at Dave's dog, who responded. That triggered Miss, who tried to dive at both at once.

A few snarling seconds later, we had them all separated and panting loudly.

"Feisty," said the man.

Jumping into the conversational opening he had created, I gushed, "she's good with people, just not good with other dogs,"

The man nodded and said, "Hmph," once again.

Dave smiled in agreement. Charles looked at me and smiled encouragingly. Camilla shrugged. Conversation stalled.

"Ahem," the woman finally said. "Is there a place around here we could book in for the night?"

"You want to stay *here*?" I asked.

The man just looked at me.

The lady stepped forward and, surprisingly, bent down to pat Miss, who wasn't sure if this new human attention was more exciting than snarling at the other dogs. "Yes. We have business to take care of, but it's getting late and we won't be able to head back today."

I looked over at Dave and Charles. Dave giggled, Charles shrugged and screwed his mouth as if to say, *beats me*. Were it summer, the pace would be humming with visitors and the local inns all busy, but at this time of year Smiths Cove was mostly deserted. Most residents flew south for the winter. Those few who remained hibernated, dog-walking their main entertainment.

"I think you'll have to go to Digby," I suggested. "It's only about fifteen minutes." I pointed in the Digby direction.

I saw a movement in the narrow space between the man's cap and his sunglasses. He had frowned, and he emitted some kind of irritable grunt.

The woman gave him a look over her sunglasses.

"Thank you," she said, dismissing us.

They climbed back into the car and in a few seconds had driven off, at a noticeably more sedate pace.

"Well!" exclaimed Camilla suddenly, "I think we managed that problem quite well!"

~

This corner of Nova Scotia offers sunsets and sunrises that delight the eye with intense water-coloured skies. My home offers me a glorious view as the colours float in across the village, and the whole of the Annapolis Basin beyond.

I am a morning person. I am fond of taking my first coffee to the deck each morning, even on these colder days. In the time it takes to finish that first mug, the black sky takes on a shifting parade of colours, beginning with the deepest blue and trailing with dusty pinks. Then would come a delicate, crisp daylight blue.

No-one in the village seems to share my morning preferences, and I am left to enjoy it in wonderful silence.

But the following morning, my ritual was rudely disturbed by the familiar sound of a powerful car. I looked down towards Highway 1. To my surprise they turned off it, towards Sunset Drive and right into my driveway.

I crouched down beside the side window in the front entrance-way and watched the two strange characters emerge again. I don't know why I felt the need to crouch and hide in my own house, but so it was.

When they knocked on the door I hesitated but told myself I was being rather foolish. I slipped on a puffy jacket—I was only dressed in pyjamas and it was chilly outside. Then I opened the door.

There stood the two of them on my small entrance porch, bundled up with caps and coats, all black as they were the previous day.

"Good morning," I said softly.

"Good morning," said the woman.

"Hmph," said the man.

I decided his grunting was rude and invited reprimand. So I raised an eyebrow at him. There.

I made no move to invite them inside. Instead, I asked, "can I help you with something?"

The man surprised me by being the one to respond. He peeled off a glove, then dug into his pocket and took out a tiny notebook. He tried to flip the pages, but fingers are not nimble on Canadian winter mornings, so he nearly dropped the notebook instead. Making a grumbling sound, he pulled off the other glove and stuffed both gloves into one of his pockets.

After flipping pages back and forth for a few seconds, he squinted his eyes and nodded, evidently finding the page he was looking for. Out of the corner of my eye I saw the woman roll her eyes.

"Mushteryurkett," the man mumbled, a cloud of vapour obscuring his face.

"Sorry?" I asked

"Muster," he paused while screwing his eyes to read the rest of his note closely. "Yurkett," he finally pronounced.

"Oh." It suddenly clicked, "Urqart. My name is Urqart."

He glared at me, then turned to the woman. "Swodeyesaid," he said.

"Oh for god's sake, Frank, it's not what you said. The man's name is Urqart not Yurkett. It's hard enough understanding you at the best of times, let alone when your mouth is frozen." She attempted a conspiratorial smile at me but it made me feel very uncomfortable.

Her face was probably once attractive, but years of dieting, stress and no doubt alcohol had funnelled out the soft contours, leaving yellowed parchment skin wrapped tightly over a fragile skull. The coat hung loosely but hinted at a painfully thin body.

As her face was sharp and edgy, his was rounded and puffed. His nose was red and bulbous, and there were streaks of purple veining it.

The man took up the notebook again. "So, Mister Urekett," he growled.

I sighed but did not bother to correct him. His growl resembled blocks of ice being dragged across a kitchen grater. I imagined his throat scarred by a lifetime of nicotine. I wondered how long it would be before the two of them asked if they could light up.

He fumbled with the notebook again, his hands shaking. "Tighters init?" he said.

I didn't know much cockney slang, but I'd heard enough in my years to know he had said *Taiters isn't it?* which in Cockney meant it's dammed cold. Something to do with potatoes and mould, but to be honest you'd have to be born into cockney rhyming culture to understand it. In any case, I gathered he was making the point that it was cold outside and I hadn't invited them in.

"I would invite you in," I said pleasantly, and he looked up with interest, "but I'd like to know who you are first."

"Oh of course," the woman said, "how neglectful of us." She removed her sunglasses. "My name is Harris, Pamela Harris. This"—she gestured at him as if he were a pet—"is Cooper, Francis Cooper."

"Frank." Grunt. He followed her lead and removed his glasses then. I would very much have preferred that they both kept them on.

"Um, and you are from?" I asked.

"Interpol," she said.

"MI6," he said at the same time.

I stood my ground and raised an eyebrow. They exchanged the kind of look couples make when they make a mistake they've made many times before and somehow manage to keep repeating.

She sighed. "Actually it's both, she said. We represent both organizations."

The International Police, and Britain's foreign intelligence secret service? "I suppose you'll have identification," I said.

This brought about an embarrassed shuffle on her part. He noticed a mark on his shoe and gave it his attention.

"Retired," she said. "We are retired officers but have an interest in one or two older cases."

"I see," I said. I didn't. I made no move.

"Blimey!" Frank exclaimed with frustration. I didn't know people said blimey anymore. He started to fuss with his notebook again. "We lookin' for"—he flicked the pages, flicking the pages one way then the other—"We looking for...a...man,"

"Oh, give me strength!" Pamela shouted in exasperation. She ripped the notebook from his hands and stuffed it into her pocket. Rolling her eyes yet again, she said, "We're trying to locate someone. It's very important. He is British. English, actually. Would have moved to these parts sometime in the past five years."

She paused for a moment, giving me quite an intense look. "He would be single, and at least sixty years old." She cocked an eyebrow at me, and I cocked one back.

"Let's see"—I ticked off on my fingers—"English. Moved here sometime this past five years. Over sixty. You've really narrowed it down then, haven't you?"

She tightened her jaw, which was impressive given how tight it had been already.

Frank drew a sharp breath. "Syoo, innit?" he accused in that ravaged growl.

"It's me?" I laughed. "Congrats on your detective abilities. I'm English, single and sixty. Amazing job. Well done."

He adopted what I'm sure was meant to be a threatening scowl. It probably had been quite fearsome in his earlier days. Now it just made him look constipated.

I stepped back and put my hand on the door. I said, "Look, I don't know who you people really are, what you're doing here or why you think you've got the right to come and question me in my own home at the crack of dawn. But I think this conversation has gone far enough and I'll bid you goodbye."

I closed the door and leaned against it, waiting for my breathing and heartbeat to slow. It was not in my nature to be blunt. I tensed, expecting them to pound on the door demanding to talk again.

But instead, I heard the car doors open and close, followed by the sound of their car driving away.

~

"Did you see where they went after that?" Pete asked me.

"Yep, they didn't go far. Straight to the church, got out and started walking house to house. I heard a raised voice. Someone didn't appreciate being woken up at that hour."

Pete looked at his watch. "So they've been at it about thirty minutes."

"That's about it, yes."

Pete had always been friendly, chatty, even. But now he sat back in his chair and fixed me with a look of serious contemplation. Nobby jumped onto his lap. "And why have you come straight to me?"

"English, over sixty, single, been here maybe five years or less. If it's not me, then who?" I waited for a moment and got nothing. "And you've mentioned you were army and police?"

Nobby twitched its head between the two of us as Pete stayed silent.

"You stalked off when they arrived. I thought it was because you were annoyed with them, but maybe its because you recognized them...?"

Again he remained inscrutable. I'm pretty sure he did not blink. It was quite disconcerting.

"Well," he suddenly said, "if you can figure that out in ten minutes it won't take them too long to get there, will it?"

He stood, pushing Nobby to the floor, much to the dog's disgust. He opened a drawer and retrieved a pair of binoculars.

I followed him out the door and to the top of his small driveway. He scanned and pointed down towards Highway 1. "There they are, still going house to house. Reckon I've got an hour, maybe."

"An hour to do what?"

"Time to move on."

Abruptly he marched back into his house and disappeared downstairs to his basement.

I shouted down after him, "Pete, what is it, who are they, who are you? What do they want with you?"

He came back up the stairs carrying two suitcases. The narrowness of the staircase made it difficult for him to handle two at a time, so I reached down and took one from him. He walked straight past me to his bedroom, signalling me to follow him with a trailing finger.

He began to speak as he emptied his cupboard and drawers. "I *was* in the army, like I said. For years. Now, you probably think I wasn't the perfect physical specimen for a fighting man"—I tried to look confused—"and you'd be right. But turns out I had two attributes they really wanted. The body was one."

I frowned.

"See, I was a nimble little thing in my day. Dammed fancy gymnast. Could have been a competitor, if I wanted. They noticed it."

This"—he pointed at his head—"was the other."

He continued to pack as he talked.

"I had a knack for fixing things and taking things apart. They put me into engineering studies, and I flew through it. I could make some tricky gadget stuff. That was useful enough. But I could also get into spaces no one else could. Bottom line is, I was valuable."

He paused for a moment. "But I had enough of the army. Started feeling me age, you know? Comes a time you start to think about getting sent in where there's bullets flying, and yer nerves make you slow down a bit. So I quit. Went home to London and started thinking about what next. Then one day there's a bloke at my door. A suit."

"One of them?" I gestured with my thumb.

"Nah. He was a smart one, this. Older fella, a toff—you know what I mean?"

I nodded.

"Said he was police, but not regular police. Special Investigations, he said. Wanted me to do work for him."

"Doing what?"

He faced me for a moment. "It was the eighties," he said, "not exactly the dark ages, but they didn't have all that fancy technology there is today, like DNA, CCTV, GPS and the like."

Pete was rolling socks as he spoke. I thought of helping him, but the idea of rolling another man's socks didn't appeal. So I kept myself propped against the wall, with my arms crossed.

"Turns out, sometimes investigations got stuck. Sometimes big cases." He picked up a shirt to fold and pointed a finger in the air to emphasize a point. "Evidence," he pronounced gravely. "Sometimes they know what the evidence is, even where it is. But they can't get it. Legal stuff, warrants, you know?"

I nodded, carefully so as not to show approval.

"Then they needs a Nudger."

"Nudger" I couldn't resist asking.

He smiled indulgently. "Someone who can get in and out of tight spots, do a little of this and a little of that, and…nudge things a bit."

"Sounds like tampering."

He sighed. "Maybe. Thing is, I got a lot of cases where I got what they needed to get."

I decided it wasn't worth commenting on the morality of all this. It was his history, that's all.

"I won't lie to you," he carried on, shooing Nobby off the case he'd been packing. "I liked it. I got to use my skills without bullets flying over me head. I got to see bad guys done in. Money was good."

"Something must have happened, though, or they wouldn't be looking for you."

He nodded. "Cases started to change. International cases. Terrorism."

I raised my eyebrows.

"You were a kid in the seventies, right?"

I nodded.

"You remember how terrorism was then. PLO, Baader Meinhoff, Red Brigade, IRA, hell, even the Quebec separatists. In the eighties they were mostly fading out. But governments wanted to round up the stragglers. Make examples of them, make sure the movements were killed off good and proper. Catching old terrorists was a big-time priority."

"But I bet not a lot of easy evidence left lying around," I offered.

He grinned. "Not a lot at all. So guess who's in demand?"

"Okay, so which side were those two on?" I thumbed in the general direction of the BMW.

"That's the thing, right there."

"Excuse me?"

"Sides. That's the thing with terrorists. Sides. Keep changing, you see. Today's school bully is tomorrow's brother-in-law."

I didn't respond, but understanding was dawning.

"I seen stuff, I know stuff. Stuff they don't want seen and known anymore."

"So they want to kill you?"

To my surprise he laughed out loud. "What, those two? Gimme a bit of credit, lad. Those two are retired operatives. Used me for a big case of theirs. Made big progress that way"—he gestured with a straight arm in one direction—"and then some deal happens and its turned all the way around that way," he swivelled around to point the other way.

"And what do you know? Suddenly there's some important folk standing this side that used to be standing that side."

"And you know who was standing where and what they were up to when they were."

He screwed his eyes as he chewed through my tortured sentence, then grinned and said, "Heh! I actually think you nailed it."

"And they want to make sure you never let your secrets out."

"Yep."

"But they don't want to kill you?"

"Oh no, they want something more important to me than that. They want my anonymity."

"I'm lost again."

"That gent that made me the offer? The Toff?"

I nodded.

"He was a proper professional. We both knew he was asking me to take on work that could land me in big trouble one day. So he made me a deal. Every job would come to me directly from him, or in a safe drop. Apart from him, not a single person would ever meet me or see me. And it worked. I did jobs for them for twenty years or more, off and on. I got to know lots about them and their operatives. But to them I was just a code name. They never saw me, never had a picture of me on file."

"So those two don't even know who they're looking for?"

"Nope. Why do you think they'd suspect you? They've tracked me here for sure. But they're tracking scraps. Good detective work, getting here on scraps, I'll give them that."

"And if they catch you? What then?"

"They'll get pictures. Betcha they've got some fancy camera with zoom lenses. When they've got my identity, won't be long before they've found out things about me, my family..."

"Family?"

He just stared ahead for a moment and swallowed.

"Think you'd better be heading back now," he said after a moment. "Thank ye kindly for your warning and it's been nice knowing you. But I best finish up now and head off soon."

We shook hands, I wished him good luck and left.

~

As soon as I reached home I slipped the leash on Miss and headed down to Highway One.

I saw the black BMW parked in the church driveway. I looked around and saw Harris and Cooper standing at an open doorway about four houses down from their car. Homes are spread quite far apart in Smiths Cove, so a door-to-door operation involves some walking, which I don't suppose they enjoyed.

They were talking to a woman who was pointing into the area behind her house, the area where Pete had his house.

They ended their conversation and hurried back towards their car. I use the word 'hurried' in a very general sense. Neither of them were capable of a sprint, but they did walk at a briskish pace.

They saw me. I waved, attempting to distract them. She ignored me, he shook his head with irritation.

I glanced up towards Pete's place and saw his car reversing. They were only a minute from their car. If they drove in his direction they must surely see him driving away.

Then Dave and his dog appeared down the small walking track that ran alongside the church. He grinned and waved a greeting at the visitors. He crossed over to their car and I heard him call out, "Morning! You back again?"

They waved at him hurriedly and dismissively. She had the car keys out now. She clicked and the trunk popped open. As she clambered into the car he took something out of the trunk. An expensive camera with a lens far larger than the camera itself.

I tugged Miss and strode across the road towards them all. "Morning, Dave!" I called out, brighter and cheerier than I had ever done before.

Dave smiled and then his smile froze. He pulled at his dog's lead and tried to get the poor creature behind him.

Miss strained at her lead. Sounds like the grinding of an overworked tractor rose out of her throat.

Dave's dog lurched and he pulled hard on its lead. Both dogs erupted into a snarling, barking frenzy, with Dave and I just managing to hold them from each other's teeth.

Harris and Cooper stopped, not sure how to circle safely around to their car. They edged one way, then the other, clearly frustrated but reluctant to get too close to the frenzied dogs.

"Can't you keep your dogs apart?" she called.

I pulled an apologetic face and knelt in front of Miss, blocking access to the drivers door. I made an exaggerated show of trying to lecture Miss into submission.

While the two black-suited visitors stood watching over us with very visible irritation, I saw a movement out of the corner of my eye. Pete's car had turned east on Highway One.

It drove at a steady pace with very little engine noise. I watched as the car reached the top of the rise and disappeared over it.

"Sorry about that, Dave," I said as I pulled Miss firmly and walked away back towards my house.

Curse of the Ten

Ten hardened Digby men boarded the boat
Ten hardened Digby men sailed it afloat
Winds blew a mighty squall, one washed away
Nine hardened Digby men sailed home that day

Nine hardened Digby men sailed the next day
Nine saddened hearts prayed in peace may he lay
A wave washed up high and over a mate
Only in harbour did they find they were eight

Eight wary Digby men sailed in the morn
Men out of Digby don't bow to forlorn
When their eyes once again were all raised to heaven
A stroke to the brain took their number to seven

Seven it was who trembling filed
Hoping this day at last would be mild
But the motor broke down and needed a fix
A spark in the wires made them now only six

Five men turned up but the sixth stayed away
He sent word of fevers and rested that day
The five knew it false but did not contest it
On returning they learned that his heart had arrested

Five Digby men knew their fate was done, sealed
They prayed to their god for his or her shield
But that day the sun was burning their eyes
And one man looked up and blinded he dies

The four Digby men that remained were now lost
They knew on each day that one would be tossed
Each looked to the others with eyes dull from fear
Which ones would return and for whom shed a tear?

Those four Digby men sailed silent and slow
They no longer thought of the catch stored below
Though calm was the water they steered from each wave
Forgotten were times they were hardened and brave

Eight frightened Digby eyes stared into space
They sailed beyond range of the call of their base
Drifting in silence their minds vaguely wandered
Will all have to die? the question they pondered

In ocean deep water his splash was not heard
A second lay choked and a knife for the third
The fourth man stood over the men once his mates
Now one hardened Digby man waited his fates

The boat never found its way back to its home
Nor any known shore, though searchers did comb
Though stories were told no one ever did know
Why the Curse of the Ten did to Digby shores blow.

Loyal

In early June of 1783 we left behind New York, now in the hands of Washington's Continental Army. We headed north until, early on the fourth day, the ship's sails shifted and we turned east.

We headed to a narrow gap where two land masses poised, like a finger and thumb about to pinch on each other. I thought of the clashing rocks from the adventures of Jason and his Argonauts, and it reminded me of my mam when she had been strong and she made me read the tales of Greek legends.

I protested so much that fanciful tales were of no import in times such as these. But in secret I loved them.

My stomach contracted as we entered the passage, half expecting the water to boil as the two land fingers moved towards each other to trap us in their final touch.

But they were, after all, just grand outcrops containing an inland sea. We sailed through without trouble, and just a little further the sails were lowered as we coasted toward a nearby shore.

When the ship halted, the anchor was dropped. The crew busied themselves loosening the ties on the rowing boats. The other two ships in our convoy fanned and came to graceful stops to either side of us.

The top deck erupted in activity as passengers crowded to the starboard rail, while the officers barked and the crew scurried this way and that.

I ran below deck to the small space we had been allocated and found my Mam still lying there. "It's grand, Mam. There's un- touched land as far as the eye can see, and I swear I never did see so many trees. You must come see."

I helped her to her feet and we limped unsteadily till we reached the short steps to the deck. She had not the strength to climb them, nor I the strength to lift her. Her wee body was light, but I was only a boy of sixteen then, and mostly skin and bone myself.

Then someone obscured the light from the hatchway. "Georgie?" I heard him call.

"Aye, Billy," I shouted back. "I want my Mam to see."

There was a scuttling and then Billy Dickson was beside me. He gently took my mother's weight from me and eased her up the steps, taking care that her feet were well placed. When someone appeared, wanting to descend he shushed them away. They did as he bade them, without hesitation.

Billy helped my mother to the rail and made sure her hands were squarely placed before he let her go. I thanked him and the three of us stood together.

"It's grand indeed," said my ma. Her voice was breathless, per- haps from the exertion, perhaps from the site before her.

There was a narrow stretch of pebble beach just a short dis- tance from the ships. From there rose the land. In some places it rose gently; in others, the rise was steep. Beyond those rises, the land undulated into the distance.

The hubbub of excitement faded into silence. I could hear water lapping against the side of the ship, the busy mutterings of the ships' crews, a fluffing sound as the last of the sails dropped and a splash as the first of the rowboats dropped to the water.

"The trees," I whispered to myself.

"Aye." Billy was subdued too. "I never expected to see so many trees."

I heard someone's voice call, "It'll all need clearing afore we can build. And a winter coming an' all."

Everyone looked at him then turned their sober eyes to the shore again, where the trees blanketed every inch of land beyond the beach, like a giant species of lichen.

"I believe we have a few months before the winter tests us, sir," came a voice, commanding and confident. Admiral Sir Robert Digby himself, resplendent as always in his blue.

We all turned from the rail to give him our attention. But he frowned at us and said, "I have nothing more to say. There is work to be done."

He turned to his officers. "Signal the other ships. We shall require able-bodied men to form scouting parties. They are to take weapons and fan out in pairs." He glanced at his fob watch. "Let us give them, say, six hours to explore and return. That will be around sunset. All others are to remain on the ships."

Billy was called to join the landing party as a scout. He patted me on the shoulder as he left. "No time for worryin' now, Georgie-boy. You get yer Mam settled and rested now."

But I thought of that forest, and I thought of how it fell on me to fashion a home for me and my Mam, or she would die this winter, and maybe me with her. I thought, *What had my fifteen years of scrapping on the streets of New York done to ready me for this?*

~

Billy told me there were a few clearings here and there where some New England planters had built huts many years ago, but most of the land would be for clearing ourselves. I didn't want him to think me weak, so I showed him a face that was serious and thoughtful, and I hoped it showed confidence.

Days passed, then finally other passengers were allowed to leave the ship. A rush of people crowding the boat stations, and the sailors at the boats lashed out with bully sticks until the passengers calmed and waited in turn.

I took the third round of transfers, leaving my Mam on board, as comfortable as I could make her in our tiny allotment below deck.

Most of the white passengers had taken the first and second rounds, so I found myself with some of the black folk who had been squeezed into tight spaces between the cargo in the storage decks. They must have been even wearier than the white folk, but they showed none of it. They were excited and full of smiles.

They nodded to me and I nodded back, but I kept my silence. They probably thought me arrogant, but I was simply lost in my own worries.

~

Admiral Digby addressed us all on the beach, and outlined his plan. My fears were eased. We would all work together to clear an area of its trees and use those logs to construct large common cabins, where we would spend our first winter together. The scouts had identified places where clearing and building would be easiest. No individual land would be granted until the winter had passed.

This brought protests from some of the genteel folk. The Admiral raised his hand and demanded silence. It was a mark of his leadership that they all obeyed immediately.

"We are twelve hundred souls. I have not led you here to preserve one or two hundred only. In the spring of next year, ships will arrive from England stocked with supplies, building materials, clerks and magistrates. Then we will begin to form a regular society with all due status and ownership properly recognized."

The objectors seemed mollified.

"But until then, we will come together that we may survive together. We will act as a community where the life of one has equal import to the lives of all."

There were some glances towards the mass of black people standing together at one side of the gathering. There must have been a couple hundred of them. But no-one spoke out. These were the fighting men of the Black Pioneers and their families. They had fearsome reputations as soldiers.

Though I was only sixteen, I was put among the men to work, and I was glad of it. Mam had pushed me towards books. She insisted if I could read and write, if I could use numbers and know some law, history and science, I would have a chance to make something of myself one day.

I did not question her on it, but I was equally glad to learn some practical skills and build some muscle onto my wiry frame. I felt this new country of ours would demand as much of my body as it ever would my mind.

June was hot and humid, as it would have been in New York. But in New York I could rest where the alleyways acted as funnels that cooled the warm breezes. Here in Nova Scotia, we worked in constantly cloying air.

I thought an axe would be easy to wield, but my first attempts ricocheted off the tree trunks and sent a frightful pain flashing through my arms and shoulders. Once or twice I lost control of the handle and curses rained down on me from those my axe narrowly missed. Once, one of the men made to rush at me, ready to swing his own axe, but Billy stepped in and he backed away.

Billy began to teach me. He showed me the proper way to set my feet, how to hold the axe with its head properly aimed, and to see the strike in my head before I let my arms swing. With his help, I became adept.

When trees were cut, I had to do my share of hauling, too. My little stick body wasn't well suited to that. But to my great delight, little bulges of muscle emerged, and my flesh lost its unhealthy pastiness.

Some men and women were formed into hunting parties. They went out every day, attempting to fill the Admiral's insatiable quota. All the other women would strip the carcasses, hanging the flesh to dry and curing the skins.

The admiral made sure we ate well each day, as we needed our strength. But most of the meat was salted and rowed over to the ships to be stored in the cargo holds. The coming winter shadowed all our activities now.

One of the gentry was Mister Cambridge. He was not happy and became vocal about it. He besieged the Admiral's tent frequently. We heard his voice protesting that gentlefolk were being made to sweat and toil as if they were commoners. Once, I heard him shout at the admiral, "For what purpose have you given passage to slaves, if not to serve their betters?"

But Digby held firm. He told Cambridge the blacks were freemen who enjoyed the king's grants the same as any white man.

Mr. Cambridge was more than angry when he strode out the admiral's tent. I think he would have taken a pistol to Admiral Digby if he were not surrounded by so many common folk.

Despite his protests, he and his family were put to manual labour the same as all others. But I noticed that, in the evenings, Mr. Cambridge huddled with his fellow gentry, and that their conversations seemed agitated at times.

June became July and then August, and in September we finally felt freshness in the morning air and a pleasant chill at night. We lit fires and sat around them.

I discovered that it is a singular pleasure to sit around a fire in the open air, exchanging stories and sometimes singing songs. Our fires were spread out across the large area we had cleared. We fell to a habit of sitting with the same people we worked with in the daytime, and so we became small, tight-knit groups. Even some of the gentry eventually dropped their guards and mingled as if they had always been our comrades.

We all had stories to tell about the war. Listening to the ones who were soldiers, I learned that war is a work of lunacy. Men wore bright uniforms so they were easy to target, and walked steadily towards oncoming fire so there was time to be shot, and they thought there was logic and heroism in this.

One night I sat next to Sergeant Thomas Peters, the man who led the contingent of ex-slaves. He was a likeable man whose quick humour was always welcome on those hot, tiring days. In serious conversation, he was unhurried and thoughtful.

One night, in the fire's embrace, I asked him a question that vexed me. If the Continentals had been fighting for liberty, why had Thomas and his people fought against them, for the King? Surely, liberty was their fight as well?

He stared at me for a while. I think he was judging if I was sincere. Then he said, "You think the men in blue just won a war for liberty?"

I shrugged. "Seems that way."

"Liberty for all?"

"Aye."

"And my people?" he then asked.

"I don't understand."

"Before this….liberty, my people were the property of those men who risked their lives to oppose oppression. But they never offered no liberty to their slaves."

I didn't say anything. I had not thought of this, and it made me feel bad that I had not.

"Do you know," he continued, "that, in the peace settlement, these newly free Americans demanded the return of all slaves in territories held by the British? Slave property, they call us."

I shook my head. I hadn't known that, either. "So will it be different here, with loyalists?"

"Ah, here we have a bargain. With the king, no less. We bargained our bodies for his armies in return for our freedom and equality when the fight was over."

A satisfied smile crossed his face. "Here we will have land just the same as the white folk. For that we have the king's promise."

~

There were evenings when rum was smuggled from the ships and passed around. Then, arguments might break out.

One night one of the men proposed a toast to the rebels' eternal torture. "In fact," he slurred, "may they have long lives festering in poverty before they burn in hell for eternity"

There were some "hear hears," but my friend Billy spoke softly.

"They were friends once, neighbours. Family for some."

The mood around the fire turned edgy. Some nodded at Billy's words. Others bristled.

"They took up arms against the law!" someone shouted. "And how many of our friends and family died for that?"

"Aye, and we killed many of them. Is that not predictable when men choose to fight? When the dust is all settled at last, who's to say which was hero and which was villain?"

Someone else spoke up. "Billy Dickson, you sound like a sympathizer."

Billy glared at him and I thought, *I would not want Billy to glare at me like that.*

"I fought," he said in a deceptively low voice that carried a threatening tone, "unlike some here who never saw a drop of blood these seven years." He paused and some faces turned away. "I donned red because my family was burned, and I hated the continentals for it." His voice choked. "But I came to know there were burnings on both sides, and in red and in blue there were bad men and good."

The toaster sneered at Billy, "Would you have us join them, then? Be one of their pathetic little states?"

"Aye, why not?" Billy answered and there were a few gasps.

I gasped, myself. I patted his leg to warn him he be cautious, for I feared this would not go down well.

But he flicked away my hand and continued. "Would that be so bad? This new country of ours, Nova Scotia, it could be the fourteenth state. Why not? Do we not have much in common?"

In the corner of my vision I saw Thomas Peters. He shook his head slowly and rose. He made his way out of the circle and headed back to where his people were camped.

Then Frederick Adams stood with a cry. On unsteady feet he crossed to where me and Billy sat. He stood over us and we cringed because he stank, and his flesh was spattered and ribboned with weeping wounds.

"You'd find us common with them, would ya?" He sprayed us with spittle as he spoke. "Me and my Emily was tarred and feathered in the streets, after their peace agreement, when we was supposed to have safe passage to our ships. I live with this"—he gestured to his wounds—"and my Emily can't yet bear to even leave the ship, so scarred she is and so ashamed to show her face."

His face by now ran with tears and his voice cracked. "Don't you tell me about making futures with the likes of them."

I willed Billy to stay silent. He did so. We both knew Frederick Adams had been an informer on his neighbours and was punished for it, but it was not the time to argue truths and perceptions.

~

Our tasks became more urgent as the days shortened and the air chilled. Rain and winds began to break our sleep as we lay in our crude shelters. We hastened the construction of the great cabins, a central meeting hall and, of course, a chapel.

We had the women and children digging up soil to make daubing that we packed into the gaps between the logs. But we lacked manure and straw in the mix. Experienced men shook their heads and muttered it would not last and we would suffer for it if the winter was harsh.

I lost count of the days I spent away from my Mam, who remained on ship with others who could not work. Whenever a boat came ashore from the ships I inquired after her and was assured she fared well enough.

I cannot say how much the gentry had suffered during the war. I'm sure they did in their own way, though they never gave the appearance of it. But for us common folk, those were indeed hard times, and we all had a different kinds of toughness bred into us by them.

With no father and a sickly mother, I myself had scraped on the streets since I was a lad of less than ten. For small coins I ran errands. I picked pockets, helped smugglers in the dead of night, fought with my fists, and even satisfied panting gentlemen in the alleys behind the taverns if the coin was right. I fancied myself a survivor, and with these months of hard labour gifting me added muscle, I figured myself ready for the worst that winter could bring.

That was naïve of me.

The remainder of our people were brought to land and given space in the large halls we had built. I was reunited with my Mam just before the last days of autumn mildness gave way to bitter winter chills.

Our crude cabins of fastened logs bore the brunt of the winds that screamed at us from the north east, and the snows that fell from late November. The old heads were right about the daubing.

It was brittle and weak and held the winds only for a short while before it cracked and flaked away. The imperfect lines of the logs left many gaps, and once the daubing was gone the wind bullied its way through those gaps.

We stuffed them with anything we could spare. Many of the furs that had been cured went into our walls instead of on our bodies. Every cabin burned its fires, and the piles of firewood shrank at a rate that alarmed us all, so that Admiral Digby was forced to assign more men to venture into the woods even in conditions that hacked at a man's courage.

I took my turns on those expeditions. Although I now wielded an axe as skilfully as any man, I struggled to hold the handle, my fingers were so numb.

We managed to keep a supply of wood, but we burned at a much faster rate, and the new wood was wet and burned badly.

Every morning we woke to the sight of crystal-bright snow covering everything we could see outside our cabins.

Days when the snow was thick but the air was still were gifts. On those days we could move around, warm our bodies, and be more productive with logging. But the wind could whip up and bellow in no time, and then we huddled like frightened animals.

A melancholy settled on some, who seemed to lose the will to look out on another blustering morning. In these days I learned that a frail heart and mind could be more vulnerable than a frail body.

When we thought we might have seen our way through the worst, our new home reminded us not to take it for granted. In February and March there were days when the sun shone and the sky was vivid blue, and we told ourselves the season was turning. But they were flirtations.

Even as we hoped for spring, temperatures plummeted without warning, and on some days the wind howled so strong it seemed all those days in the early winter had been just practice. We would only huddle together in our cabins, packed close together in the corners where our crude stuffings were holding.

We had landed with thirteen hundred souls, and I heard tell that our numbers had shrunk to less than one thousand by the time the winter finally relented.

The dead could not be buried or burned, so the corpses had been piled in heaps against the sides of the cabins. The piles grew so they became gruesome barriers against the wind.

My Mam lay amongst those bodies. I had tried to keep her as warm and comfortable as I could, but it was futile. I had no means to warm her but my own shivering body, and she being frail already had no strength to resist the frozen fingers of Hades.

~

Spring finally brought in warmer air and we began to venture around. The church had been blown away completely.

But the meeting hall had mostly survived, and after repairs had been made the Admiral sent word that a meeting was to be held there. Each family should send one person to attend.

Billy and I went together. We arrived a little early. There were three rows of bench seats at the front, all empty. We made for them but we were told they were reserved.

In due course, the former gentry of New York arrived at their leisure and sat themselves while the rest of us we stood.

The admiral arrived when the gentry were all seated. The hall was packed and an overflow gathered around the entrance. He sat with his senior officers at a small table placed at the far end of the meeting hall, just in front of the bench seats.

His officers called everyone to silence and the admiral stood.

He spoke well. His message was that we should take heart now.

Despite our tragic losses, we had survived the worst. Ships would be en route from England already, bringing us clothing, building materials, food and drink, plus seeds for planting and livestock for breeding. We would have a long spring and summer to build on the impressive work we had already done. The next winter would be a challenge, but one we could face better equipped and with the benefit of experience.

His words and his confident manner were a tonic for us right then.

"Now, as to land," he continued, "we shall have a commission to allocate land so that each family has its due share. That commission shall include two of my officers, plus two representatives of high standing from the former New York community. Those representatives shall be Mister Evans, and Mister Cambridge."

There were "hear hears!" from the front rows, but mutterings from the common folk in the rest of the hall. Someone called out, "Who chose them?" but the question was ignored.

The meeting continued for another hour or so, discussing the practical matters that required attention, such as renewed scouting, mapping, soil testing, fishing, repairs to cabins, and tapping a steady supply of water. Names were allocated to tasks, based on skills and proven abilities. The responsibility for mapping was given to folks chosen from the gentry.

~

A month or so later, new ships were anchored in the gentle sunshine that calmed the bay. Work was progressing well on clearing more land.

Another meeting was called, but this time it was Mister Cambridge who spoke.

He was most pleased to announce that the mapping committee

had been productive. A total of four hundred and twenty land parcels had been mapped, each matching the King's grant of two hundred acres of good, workable land.

There was a frenzy of excitement.

Then a man called Daniel Brown stood to ask a question. "Mister Cambridge, I beg your indulgence, but how many families are we today?"

"Ahem, the number we have at hand is, let's see"—Mister Cambridge made a pretense to look for a number he doubtless knew well—"five hundred and ten, or thereabouts."

Now a different buzz rose among those standing.

Daniel Brown spoke again. "Ah, Mister Cambridge, respectfully, how is the allotment to be decided? Who is to be among the four hundred and twenty, and what of the grants owed to those who are not?"

"Goodfellow, there is no cause for concern," answered Mister Cambridge with a smile of reason. "These allotments will be allocated on a most fair basis. The four hundred and twenty shall be distributed among the free men and their families. Those who were not born as free citizens will wait until we can begin a second phase of scouting and mapping. In the meantime, they can assist those more fortunate in the arduous tasks of clearing and construction."

There followed a wave of questions, but they were all muted. Most folks seemed not to understand what Mister Cambridge had announced but were afraid to challenge him. But not everyone had missed the casual details.

Thomas Peters pushed his way inside and all the way to the front, provoking outrage from those he pushed aside.

"'Those not born as free citizens'. That is your distinction." He pointed his finger accusingly. "You know it has only one meaning."

Mister Cambridge ignored him, resuming his seat at the table.

"You mean us, the Black Pioneers. You are excluding the families of those who were slaves."

Mister Cambridge shrugged while his fellow committee members took to consulting their papers.

"This cannot stand! We have a promise from King George." Thomas shouted.

But Mister Cambridge began to collect his papers. He waved a hand imperiously, signalling an end to the meeting.

As he walked away, he said to Thomas, "The promise made to your kind will be kept, but the allocation must of necessity be prioritized."

"Kind? Prioritized? What do those words mean?"

But Thomas was shouting at Mister Cambridge's retreating back.

~

"It's an awful wrong," I said to Billy as we walked back to our cabin. "We have to say something."

"Well," Billy mumbled.

I stopped walking and turned to face him. "Billy, you cannot tell me you agree with that?"

He looked abashed. Not a look I had seen on him before. He continued walking and didn't say anything.

"Billy!" I stood in front of him, blocking him.

He looked angry for a moment, then sighed. "Georgie, you have to understand."

"Understand what?"

"It's the way of it, Georgie."

"It's the way of it? What does that mean?"

He pulled his shoulders back and looked me straight in the eye. Defiant. "It's God's way, Georgie."

He marched off, leaving me gasping and confused.

~

I could not return to the cabin right then, for fear of running into Billy again. He was best avoided, for both our sakes.

I wandered around and found myself close to the tents where the Admiral and his officers had made their spring quarters. There was a uniformed man sitting alone on a rickety stool outside the main tent. He was hunched, as if sheltering from a non-existent wind. Then I realized it was the Admiral himself.

I turned to leave but he looked up and caught my eye. He sat upright, and I was shocked to see that he suddenly looked aged and poorly.

"Mister Dickson, is it?" he called in a tired voice.

"Duncan, sir, George Duncan."

"Ah, yes, your mother. I am sorry."

"Thank you, sir. I tried to help her, but she lacked any strength."

"I know you did."

I flushed at such a compliment from the admiral himself.

He gestured at my face. "You have the look of someone who has lost something valuable."

I felt embarrassed as I think I may have been shedding a tear. So I said nothing.

"Shall I tell you what it is, this thing you have lost?"

"Sir?"

"Your innocence."

I cast my head down.

"You thought our band of refugees would make a better world out here? You thought they would forget their greed and prejudices and miraculously love each other? You thought that here, character would matter above birth?"

I could not prevent a sob escaping, though I tried to hold it down.

He sighed. "I am sorry, Duncan. I did not mean to belittle you. You thought well of your people. There is no wrong in that. The wrong is with them that let you down."

He pointed and I turned. In the far distance we could see Cambridge and Evans.

"One year and a bit I have spent in the company of those men. I have learned more about the devious nature of man in this time than in a lifetime of service to my country."

He took in a deep breath. "They have defeated me, Duncan. I simply lack the wit to keep up with their politicking. They and theirs will govern, not the likes of me. Their holdings will grow as others shrink and none will question the legitimacy of it. They will have themselves elected by the same people they swindle, who will indeed proclaim them champions of the common man. They will be the pillars of church and society, even as they rob and fornicate and abuse. As for the Black Pioneers, I fear their case is hopeless."

"But they have friends among the white folk. We can rally to support them," I protested.

Digby looked me in the eye and shook his head, and I saw Billy's face in my mind and I knew he was right.

~

When magistrates arrived from England, the case of the Black Pioneers was petitioned and the order was given to assign them the acreage each had been promised. It was done, but the land given to them was mostly hostile and rocky outcrops with poor accessibility, useless as farmland or habitation.

Before long, many of them had left, some across the water to New Brunswick. Others, Thomas Peters included, found passage across the ocean to Africa, to a place of new hope for ex-slaves called Sierra Leone.

Many of the white settlers found it hard to clear and farm their virgin land, only recently cleared of trees and still pitted with their trunks and roots. But the waters in the bay teemed with sea life. Many families turned to fishing instead of farming their land.

The mapping commission became a council. They set taxes on unoccupied land, then confiscated the land of settlers who could not pay the taxes, and sold the land off to themselves at bargain prices.

Billy was one who had no affinity for farming, nor for fishing. But he made a deal by selling his land and invested in a public house. His gregarious nature was well suited to it, and he prospered.

I cannot say if his tavern was a good one, for I never entered it.

Admiral Digby left us shortly after the betrayal of the Black Pioneers. He returned to England, where we heard he served as a member of Parliament, as was expected of a man of his class and service.

I heard he lasted in parliament only a short time before taking retirement, and I have always imagined it a period of time he disliked intensely.

Our community petitioned the Crown to name our new town "Digby."

Virus and the City

It was the dawn of the COVID era. The world was terrified and we lived in lockdowns. Yet somehow I was summoned to a medical appointment in Halifax. I remember the trip like this:

Heading to the city I said they said wow the city that's a long drive but their eyes said the city that's so glamorous you're so lucky I wish I was with you then I tell them we will overnight in the city and have a night on the town and their eyes glow with envy and they say enjoy but their eyes say you probably won't appreciate it cause you come from the city.

The road is good but long and lined with trees and lined with trees and lined with trees and the trees fill the horizon and the space to the left and the space to the right and the trees are winter bare and the branches grasp towards the sky like old men's knotted fingers in a plea and here and there are still patches of snow and lakes still coated in places with ice and the road is winding and empty so empty and the twisting tarmac mimics the trees and stretches and pleads and why are we on this road with the road so empty then ah there's a truck heading towards us and he passes and looks down on us as he passes and his eyes say why are you on this road today there are not many like us heading to the city today.

As I approach the city the GPS lady says keep to the right lane and take the right fork to the city but it doesn't matter which lane no traffic to negotiate not many like us on the road today heading to the city today and the toll road looms do I have the right coin is the change lane open no its closed no staff in the booths today yes I have the right coin so I throw it in the basket and drive on through and cross the bridge and there is the city and the exit lane should be busy but it's free today and we breeze through and the GPS voice says keep to the left lane but it doesn't matter which lane no traffic today not many like us heading to the city today.

What kind of city is this I've never seen a city like this it should be busy with people but there's a takeaway that's closed and a coffee shop a laundromat and a supermarket and a bakery and a boutique and they are all closed no trading no money no people looking in the windows no people walking out with bags full of clothes and snacks to eat and cups to drink, there are a few people on the streets but only singles or couples no groups no loitering at crossings just walking because why not if you have nothing else to do and I open my window and the sounds should flood in like the constant hum of engines and the chatter of people and the hoots and toots and barks and calls but it's not like that today it's just empty roads today and the faint phew of a breeze as it drifts through the spaces and the spaces and the lights take long to change but then we move quickly there's no traffic today not many like us heading to the city today.

The hotel is open but the man at reception is wary as we approach you are most welcome he says but we must inform you he says no service at all but the room itself and no food will be served and no drinks to be had and it's best you know that the restaurants are closed all around all around we ask all around he says the whole city he says they are all closed all around the city he says and even the coffee shops and takeaways and where people might gather all is closed and he says he is sorry but his eyes say why did you come at all and we look to ourselves and we ask ourselves why did we come at all and we say thanks but no thanks we think we will pass on this stay and we leave.

Then to the clinic we go for the reason we came to the city today where not many like us would venture today to the clinic we go to the parking beneath and the spaces are many we park within seconds but wonder at this as the parking at clinics is always a struggle but we won't complain and we walk to the entrance two men two security men two men in uniforms and they ask us our business and tell us go right and we see the sign for the left and it's for people who need testing and there is a room where they wait for their test and the room is still and the room has a thickness and the people sit quietly no chatter among them they sit in their seats and they stare straight ahead and there are three maybe four seats between each of them they do not sit close and their eyes do not see us but the eyes say fear and the virus is here it is here for me and for me and for me and some may not believe but for me it is real.

We go to the right to the screen where we register but sanitize first and then touch the screen and then sanitize again for the sign written large says that must be done then they point us to the passage where another man waits and he asks for my name and have I travelled at all and have I been with anyone who might have some symptoms and do I myself have any signs of some symptoms I say with relief I have no signs no symptoms no contacts no worry and he smiles and says come then a little while later my appointment is done and I am cleared to leave and we walk past the front and the people to the left (now the right as we exit) and the people still sit with their stares and no chatter and their eyes still say fear and believe me it is here and we linger only to pause at a sanitizer again and we leave.

Our plan to stay in the city this day is now done and we head to the highway again and we feel rather strange as we pass through the city where not many people like us would venture today and

the highway comes quickly more quickly than ever and we drive
for some time with silence our voice and turn on the radio and
wait for some news and they say on this day six hundred more die
from Italian shores just one day just one day six hundred or more
just one place just one day and we drive more in silence and the
road reaches out and the road reaches up in a plea and the trees
the trees and the trees join the plea and the road stretches on with
us all alone as not many would venture like us today.

Christine

I don't know why it interests you, but as you insist, I will tell you my story.

I am Christine. But I am also Akua. I was born on Wednesday, and in Ghana. Akua is one of the names for a girl born on a Wednesday. My family name is Annan for my father's mother, for I am Ashanti, and the Ashanti way is to carry the maternal name.

I was born in Elmina, the place where the white conquerors of old built two great forts that still stand on the beautiful but haunted coast of Western Ghana. Those forts were the staging places for slaves captured by the warriors of the great Ashanti empire, from where they would be shipped to the New World.

The forts are tourist attractions now, where visitors only have to imagine the stench of bodies crammed together on a stone floor in their own piss and shit. My father worked as a tourist guide there. My mother ran a small bar where she served beers, plates of Jollof rice and Akpateshi.

Hah! Akpateshi is a fearsome home-made spirit common in Ghana. You would probably call moonshine, though I think Ghanaians would laugh at your moonshine.

Both my parents earned decent incomes, and that elevated us a little from the fishing families that surrounding us. I was able to complete my schooling all the way through high school.

Then a day came when I set off in a minibus taxi on a four-hour journey to Accra, where I would attend the University of Ghana in Accra. I was unsure of myself and foolishly stood back, allowing others to board the van before me. I found the only seat left to me was a half seat on the aisle, the other half of the seat occupied by the overflowing bulk of a man squeezed into the window seat. His eyes were already closed and the beginnings of a snore farted from his nose.

I spent the four hours trying to find a comfortable way to twist my body while avoiding the eager fingers of a young man seated behind me who thought himself charming to a young country girl travelling alone.

I was relieved when the van reached the western reaches of Accra, and I was one of the first to exit when the driver called out, "Jamestown."

I was to stay in Jamestown with my cousin Amah, who shared a room above a store there with her friend Abina.

Jamestown. Who hasn't heard of it? But hearing its stories didn't prepare me for it. I stepped out of the taxi with my bag in my hand and I froze.

The driver had dropped me in front of the huge red and white lighthouse that overlooked the beach and ocean. I was glad of that, as Amah had arranged to meet me right there, and I would not have found the courage to venture from that spot on my own.

All around me was a frightening blur of sound and movement. The main road was choked with cars in both directions, men, women, and even children scurrying in between them without fear or consideration. Cars hooted and voices cried out. Motorcycles dashed past the cars, leaping onto pavements as they pleased and hooting at pedestrians to leap out of their way.

I looked down the road that snaked ahead of me and saw buildings after buildings. Some looked solid, with doors and windows and flaking paint. Some were just fragile shacks. New and old, strong and fragile, they were all squeezed impossibly beside each other and on top of each other as if they were building blocks that some god had one day cast down in a bored fit.

Jamestown is just a tiny wedge of land in Southwestern Accra. Probably half the size of Digby's centre. Probably no more than a few hundred were ever expected when the colonial English first built the lighthouse and settlement. Now, eighty thousand survive a tough, hard-paced existence there.

Do you know what the average income is, even today? Less than one hundred dollars a month. Imagine surviving on that!

There are hundreds of tiny shops that sell only a handful of things. This one sells toiletries, that one cleaning materials, this one canned goods. There are hundreds of tiny restaurants and bars, some no more than a counter and a single plastic table with four plastic chairs around it. Others are larger, with music and a TV to show the English soccer, because English soccer is life, isn't it?

There are stalls spilling onto the pavements, selling vegetables and fruits. Butchers hang slabs of meat in open windows, attracting clouds of flies, but no one is deterred by the flies.

I waited for about ten minutes, but it seemed like hours. I clutched my bag so tightly to my chest. Every person who passed me looked like they would snatch it from me.

Then I heard Amah's voice screaming my name from across the road. Her face was lit, she jumped up and down with her hand waving and she called me over.

I didn't think I could cross that road, but a woman started to cross right beside me, so I tucked in behind her, tracking her as she snaked and ducked and gestured at drivers who crowded her space. I thought I could never learn to do that.

~

Over the next two years I grew into that Jamestown chaos. I learned that clutching a bag tightly isn't a smart way to avoid attention, that the only rule of the road that matters is to spot a gap and take it. Hesitation only confuses other pedestrians and drivers.

I learned to deal with the constant catcalls and occasional gropes from men in the streets with a roll of the eyes, a jerking arm and a drop-dead, "You wish." I learned how to press for a bargain but to always respect the seller and always call her madam. I learned which taxi drivers were safe and respectful and I learned to reward them with a smile and a wave as they dropped me where I needed to be.

The heart of Jamestown was the open-air boxing ring. No matter how urgent the need for more living spaces, Jamestown had kept just enough clear space around the boxing ring to cram in a couple of thousand cheering fans, body to body to body.

Every time a big ship from Russia or China or America docked at Accra, crowds would gather, knowing the ship's best would make their way to Jamestown to test themselves against the local champions. Jamestown produced champions of Africa and even one world champion.

The day after I arrived, Amah showed me around Jamestown, and when we walked around the boxing square she told me to steer clear of the boxers, as they think themselves idols to the local girls.

"But they are just local boys and offer nothing," she said, and when I puzzled her words she told me I would see that Friday night.

I moved into Amah's place with her and her friend Abina. The little flat was up a flight of rusty stairs above a shop that sold second-hand clothing.

Amah and Abina explained how this made the flat sought-after.

No stinking meat or loud-mouthed drunks below us, they said.

The flat was small for two people and cramped for three. Still, they had been so nice. They had taken old sheets and hung them so they divided the place into three spaces.

I had a mattress of my own and a small set of drawers to store my things. When I first saw the space I had to make an effort not to cry and seem ungrateful.

But I came to be comfortable.

~

On that first Friday, Amah and Abina took me to Rockstones, where the music is loud and the lights flash red and blue, and there are booths with round tables surrounded by seats of thick white leather. A single drink cost more than all the money we had in our purses together.

Amah and Abina dressed in tight dresses with high hems and low cleavage, and I felt embarrassed by my country clothes. But they told me not to worry. They said I had the face and the figure, and before we set off they helped me alter my plain dress to make it more revealing.

I felt self-conscious and a little vulnerable, for I had never dressed that way before.

Rockstones had only a few tables still empty when we arrived. I may have been a country girl, but I noticed the impact we three made as we entered.

Within minutes of sitting ourselves at one of the booths, we were approached by a couple of good-looking young guys, but Amah and Abina ignored them and slouched back, pretending to be busy on their phones. We sat without a drink and I grew nervous, sure that soon someone would ask us to leave, but the girls were unconcerned.

Then two middle-aged white men walked into the bar, and my companions immediately sat themselves up, adjusting their tops to make sure their cleavages displayed well.

The two men ordered drinks at the bar and right away began to look around the tables. One of them saw our table and the girls flashed smiles at him.

The man came over. I felt myself go rigid. He was mostly bald but with those little greying patches of hair above both ears that seemed a pointless vanity. He wore a lightly-checked long-sleeved shirt with button-down collar, and the cuffs buttoned, too.

I thought of the American TV shows I had grown up watching and decided he was the quiet accountant whose role in the show was to nitpick at the heroes.

But there at our table in Rockstones he had a confident swagger and a player's leer, waving his hand imperiously to a waiter to bring drinks for the girls.

He moved on to another table after a time, but took with him Abina's phone number.

That night we went on to Badu's and Clear Spice, where the routine was similar. I found it hard to play along and kept to myself when the girls flirted with the rich white guys.

Amah and I finally made our way home at around two am. Abina was no longer with us. She returned only in the late morning and went straight to her mattress to sleep.

I must have shown my disapproval, and Amah eventually turned on me. She told me I was judging her and Abina and I must stop being a prudish country girl.

I cried and then she cried and we made up.

"If you make them feel like they're exciting and attractive, they'll buy you drinks, food, whatever you want. Most times all it costs is a bit of flashing and feeling up." She tried to assure me, but I felt even more nervous.

In the evening Amah asked Abina if she had got a gift and she smiled and opened her purse, where I spied a wad of notes.

I never played their game. My parents always made sure I had money to keep me, and I didn't much enjoy the noise and flash of the club scene anyway. But Amah and Abina went off every Friday and every Saturday. Most times they returned together, a little loud and a little drunk. Sometimes one or the other didn't come back, occasionally both.

On weekends I always kept my sheet closed and pretended to be fast asleep when they arrived. But I never questioned either of them again, I always greeted them brightly the next morning, and we became easy with each other's lifestyles.

~

There was always talk about America. An American visa was the ultimate dream for most students at the University. There were agents who advertised to find graduates jobs with work permits in America.

Why America? I would argue. What's so great? All I read about was shootings and racism and fascist flags and black people being killed by white cops and riots. And what about Kwame, and Afua and Kojo? I would ask. Didn't we give them such big send-offs, like they were heroes? And didn't their families boast of the money they sent home, but the money stopped coming and their mothers are sick with worry.

Canada was my dream. My friends laughed and said I would turn to a block of ice as soon as I stepped off the plane, that Ghanaian blood wasn't made to stand a Canadian climate. But I didn't care.

When Darren's face appeared on my app I noticed the tiny Canadian flag in the bottom corner and I paused instead of swiping. I thought his eyes were kind.

I read his profile and he interested me. He was a little old, but thirty-five wasn't unbearable. He was a partner in a beer company. He lived in a city called Halifax, and when I googled Halifax I thought it a pretty city.

His profile said he wanted "a genuine person, a tender soul. Honest and kind, but with an adventurous heart." He offered love, loyalty and respect, but also romance and excitement.

I wondered how he would react to a dark girl from West Africa, but I clicked anyway.

The next year was our courtship. I needn't have been concerned about his reaction to a Ghanaian girl. From the very first messages we exchanged he gushed about how beautiful I was. Not *beautiful for a black girl*. Just beautiful.

His messages often had a hint of self-deprecating humour that I found sweet.

He asked me for pictures, but not once did he suggest nudes. He sent me pictures of his car and his home. He lived in a house, not an apartment. He jokingly called his house old and grumpy, but it was comfortable and it was home.

He told me about the brewery and their ambitions to grow. He admitted he was a bit of a workaholic but trying to find balance.

We shared our likes and dislikes. He was really interested in me. He found my American skepticism amusing, but said he shared it.

We took our conversations off the app before long and started texting and emailing. When I could find free wireless we would video call, but our internet wasn't too good in Jamestown and the video quality was always poor.

I found those calls stressful and I preferred using text and pictures.

He said love first. I opened a text message and the words seemed to be in three dimensions, bursting from my phone's screen.

I think I'm falling in love.

I held the phone in my hand and my lungs suddenly couldn't fill.

Amah looked up from her sewing. She told me I looked like I had seen a spirit. All I could do was hold the phone for her to look at it.

She shrieked and called Abina to look. Then they were both shrieking and hugging me and congratulating me. Then they were chanting, "Canada, Canada" and I was only thinking, how do I respond to the man who has just gifted me his heart?

I didn't finish my degree. I didn't mind as much as you'd expect. Darren told me he could find me a job in Halifax that would qualify me for a work permit, and after a while I could study for free at a university there. He wanted me with him to make a life together.

I travelled home to my parents. I told them about Darren and I showed them his messages and I spoke about the perfect life we would have together in Canada, and my mother wept and my father put his arm around her shoulder and he asked me only one question: "Will you be happy?"

And I had never loved my father more than I did then.

I have been talking for some time. Are you still interested? Okay, I will continue.

My journey took me from Accra to Amsterdam, where I was overwhelmed by the size of the airport. I had to find a connecting terminal and I panicked, thinking it impossible.

But to my surprise, the signs were easy to understand and I found my terminal with time to spare. From there I flew all the way across the ocean to Toronto and then connected back to Halifax.

I got lost in the different time zones and my body clock was confused. But I couldn't sleep at all, even in the six hours I waited on a surprisingly-comfortable bench seat in Amsterdam's airport.

When I arrived in Halifax I was anxious and tired. My jaw was so tightly clenched that I struggled to answer the customs officer at the immigration counter. He frowned at me and repeated his question. "Are you here to work?"

I struggled with his accent and wasn't sure how to answer. I gave him a tired smile and mumbled an apology.

Then I found the work permit Darren had sent me and passed it over with another smile, and the customs officer smiled at me and stamped my passport with a wink.

I thought of Amah and Abina then.

Darren wasn't in the arrival hall. I watched my fellow passengers meet their loved ones or business contacts until the airport fell quiet and I stood alone in this strange place.

I told myself he must have been delayed. The traffic. Surely the traffic was at least as bad and unpredictable as in Accra? But an hour later he had not appeared.

I found a bench and sat on it. I took out my phone. I didn't know then that the airports here offer free wifi, so I used my valuable contract data and sent a quick message:

    waiting at airport

But there was no reply.

I found the washroom and hid there for a while, trying to think of what to do. Only then I thought I should have had a plan in place in case things went wrong.

I emerged from the washroom more nervous than before. I knew I couldn't just wait at the airport but I didn't know where to go.

I thought about the small stash of dollars I had exchanged at the bank in Accra. I didn't know if I could use American dollars in Canada.

I felt a light tap on my shoulder.

A lady wearing a Starbucks shirt stood there. I could see the Starbucks counter behind her. She looked at me kindly. She told me she had seen me waiting around and asked me if I was lost.

Lost? I thought about it and concluded I was, so I nodded and a felt a tear on my cheek.

She reached out and hugged me. Don't worry, she told me. Don't worry.

I slept on a sofa in Daphne's apartment that night. The next morning she woke me with coffee and a plate of eggs and bacon. She showed me her bathroom, where I showered and dressed. I offered her money, but she shook her head and pushed by hands away.

Her kindness made me tearful, but she wrapped her arms around me again. She held me tightly and I felt her hand move against my back and I stiffened.

She released me and gave me a smile that seemed a little sad, and I did not understand, but still I felt a little sad, too.

Daphne called me a taxi. I was embarrassed to tell Daphne I hadn't asked Darren for his home address. But I remembered the name of Darren's brewery and the taxi driver knew of it.

Daphne had swapped me some Canadian dollars for my American so I could pay the taxi.

Daphne's apartment was in Dartmouth, and fortunately the brewery was just north of Dartmouth, so I had enough for the fare.

I stood outside the brewery with mixed feelings. I was relieved. I was a world from Ghana in a city I did not know and had been left stranded by the man who loved me. But at least here was a place that was real as it was supposed to be.

I walked inside to find a bar. A girl about my age stood behind the bar and greeted me with a wonderful smile and a breezy, "Hey, how are you today?"

I felt self-conscious at this and didn't know the appropriate response. All I could do was give her a tight smile in return and move closer to the bar.

I asked her if I could speak to Darren.

She still smiled but her eyebrows burrowed a little. "Darren, Darren Clark?" she asked me, clearly puzzled.

I nodded and she asked me to wait, disappearing through a door behind the bar.

She returned a few minutes later and told me Darren was busy cleaning tanks and I didn't know what that meant. But she told me I could wait and pointed at one of the empty tables. She brought me a glass of water and asked if I needed anything else and I said thank you but no.

Sunlight from the front window bathed the booth where I sat. My stressed and sleep-deprived body had no resistance to it, and I drifted to sleep.

I awoke as a shadow moved into the sun's patch. I looked up and shielded my eyes.

Darren stood over me, but not my Darren. This version of Darren was shorter and heavier in the middle than my Darren. His hair was thinning, but grown long at the back, where he wore it in a ponytail. His face was too lined for a man in his mid-thirties. He wore rubber Wellington boots and a denim overall pulled over a plain tee shirt.

I mumbled his name as a question.

He looked anxious and kept glancing at the girl at the bar. I wondered if he had a relationship with her but when I looked back at her she seemed as cheerful as ever and paid no attention to him. No, he was embarrassed and worried what she was thinking.

But why? He was an owner, why would he worry about the opinions of an employee?

Then he said, "Akua, you're here." Just that, as if my presence was a surprise, as if he hadn't asked me to come, as if he hadn't been excited when I sent him my flight details. As if I was not the love of his life.

I believe I started to cry then. I don't think I was loud, but the girl at the bar noticed and she went through the back door again.

Darren began to shift from one foot to another. He looked at his feet and mumbled to himself, not to me, and he wasn't coherent but some of his words found me, words like forgot, didn't expect, just talking, app, didn't mean.

The girl appeared with another man whom she introduced as the owner. He said something sharply to Darren, who nodded and hurried away past the bar and through the door.

The man said he was sorry and I asked him for what. He gestured towards the door and asked if Darren had caused trouble again and I thought, *again*?

I held my head in my hands and tried to collect myself, then I reached in my purse and extracted the work permit. I showed it to the man and asked if this was real, did the place exist?

He frowned but said yes, so I gathered my things and thanked him. I asked the girl how I could call a taxi and she hurriedly got on the phone and called one for me.

My place of work was called The Palace. The flashing neon sign outside read 'Restaurant and Nightclub'.

The Palace served food and drinks and played music. Therefore it was technically right to call itself a restaurant and nightclub. It was in a part of town filled with derelict industry, tired old shops and some neglected houses spotted around.

When I walked inside with my bag in hand I was stopped by a man who wore sunglasses, which I found odd given the dim interior, lit only with a soft red glow.

I showed him my work permit and he looked me up and down. His inspection was slow and intrusive. He then returned my permit and pointed to a door in the far corner.

There I found the owner, who looked me up and down just as slowly, then asked me if I had just arrived from Africa. I nodded and he asked me if I had anything else to wear, something tight, he said.

I shook my head and he shouted to the door. The door opened and the man gave instructions to a woman who appeared. The man told me to make myself comfortable, pointing to a large, thickly-upholstered couch against the wall in his office.

The door opened again just a few minutes later and the woman passed a bag to me, then left and closed the door. I held the bag and the man gestured impatiently at me.

I opened the bag and a white dress was inside. The man told me to put it on. I asked if there was somewhere I could change and he laughed and told me not to waste his time. Did I want the job or not?

I was afraid, but more afraid of walking into the street outside.

I took off my jeans and shirt, and as quickly as I could slipped on the tiny white dress.

The man appraised me and shook his head. It would not work with the underwear on, he told me. I had to strip off the dress, remove my bra and panties as he watched and pull on the dress again.

Then he grinned. He reached out a hand and tweaked my nipple. "Much better," he said. "Now I can see them."

The dress was too small for me, but that was no accident. Most of the girls who worked at The Palace wore similar dresses of black. But my skin was black, so they chose a white dress for me so my charcoal nipples would show well through the thin fabric.

The Darren I thought I knew was the owner of a brewery, a man of influence, a man whose connections secured my job offer. This new, horribly real Darren was just a low-life who frequented the Palace whenever he could afford it. The Palace employed girls from any part of the world, as long as they were exotic. There were Russian girls, Chinese, Filipina, an Indian girl and two girls who had the toffee skin of mixed blood.

And me. Ebony in white made near transparent in the red interior.

I had to tell them I had no place to stay, so they gave me a tiny room at the back that had a single bed and a pole stretched above it for hanging clothes. They gave me one month to find a place.

The owner came to me the first night, after all the customers had left. I cried as he took my virginity but as he wiped himself off he told me to be happy, I would be ready for customers now.

The security guy was next, coming to me in the morning before the place opened. He told me to be nice, I would need him to look after me now.

The customers were told not to touch the girls, but who stopped them when they fondled my breast as they pushed a dollar into my cleavage, or slid their hands between my thighs as I put their drinks on the table?

Are you okay? Do you want me to stop? You look uncomfortable....
Okay, I will carry on.

I finally found my way to Digby. That was Daphne's doing. I went back to her.

I made a little money from tips at The Palace and I had learned how to make the tips bigger, though it made me feel dirty. But it was never enough for me to pay for a place of my own.

I wanted to go home to Ghana, but I needed money for a ticket.

In the meantime, my boss wanted me out of the back room.

I knocked on Daphne's door and she opened the door to me without a single question. I let her hug me again.

One night soon after, I arrived home at around two am and I found her asleep on the couch, a bottle of wine half consumed on the table beside her. I woke her and in her half-sleep she told me she would stay on the couch and I should use her bed.

When she came to the bed later, I let her in, and when she kissed me and touched me I let her, for she was kind to me and what did it matter anyway?

Daphne told me her sister's ex-husband had a restaurant in Digby. A regular restaurant, she said. She'd told him about me and he was willing to give me a job, even if it was just a few months until I could afford a ticket, before my work permit expired. And Digby is a cheap place to live, she told me. You won't struggle to survive like you have here.

And so I am here.

Daphne's ex brother-in-law is David. He smiles a great deal, he pays fairly. The tips are small compared to the Place, but David lets me keep them and I don't have to give him a cut.

He hasn't put a hand on me, but he watches me a lot when he thinks I don't see, and he frequently reminds me that his apartment is right above the restaurant, should I need anything. He always says the word *anything* twice, the second time with emphasis.

The men who come to the restaurant in Digby are not like the city men who skulked into the Palace, where for a night they could put aside their corporate family man identities and behave like brutes in the company of other brutes.

Here in Digby, the men are townsfolk who come with their wives or their girlfriends and sometimes with groups of friends.

There are other girls serving at the restaurant. They are local girls and they are cute and the guys look at them. They flirt and they make a joke of it when their woman says hey.

Sometimes the men come in groups of friends. Then they all look at the girls together and they laugh together and they tell each other what they'd like to do with the girls. But not when I serve them.

Oh, they still look. But they are more careful with it. They fake distractions so they won't be seen looking. They look with their eyes and take care to hold their heads steady so it's not obvious.

Out here it's a hard thing to explain to friends that you checked out that girl with skin so dark it ain't natural.

But there are men who want more than a look. I see their hunger. One guy always takes a risk to gaze at me when he thinks his companions are not looking. He makes excuses to use the washroom so he can pass my station and catch my eye. He fumbles when taking the bill so his finger can graze mine.

So, one time I passed a note with his bill and on the note I wrote my number and beneath it I wrote one hundred dollars, and underlined it. And he phoned me that very night.

Didn't you?

Digby's Grace

The headphones and raised hoodie were just props, really. Meant to put off attempts at conversation, but anyway redundant. The girls who shared the apartment with Justine made no attempt to wake up at six am as Justine let herself out, and Digby's main street was always deserted this early. Still, she felt better with them on.

She didn't need to run at six. She only needed to be at the office at nine, and even then hardly anyone noticed when she eased into her corner desk at the Digby municipal building.

She didn't run to keep in shape, either. She couldn't care less if she fitted some kind of image template.

She ran because it used up time. She'd been an early riser as long as she could remember. If she didn't run she'd have time before the office was open and people had a way of invading idle time.

She took her usual route down to the end of Water Street, past the second-hand shops, the discount stores and the fast food joints with their tacky signage and dated neon. She turned into Racquette.

She liked to watch the threads of light shimmering on the gentle waters of the Annapolis Basin as she made her way onto Shore Road.

She'd been reminded many times that its sweeping curves invited speeders, and without a curb it wasn't advisable for a sole jogger in the early morning half light. But she didn't care.

She followed Shore around the bay until she reached the Digby Pines resort. There she rested and let the sunrise warm her before she headed back.

Turning back into Water Street was the usual disappointment. She'd seen old photographs in the municipal offices that showed Digby had once been handsome and elegant. But years of weak town management had turned it into an unattractive strip of cheap commerce and ugly square buildings.

But something caught her eye, a flower. It was close to the opposite curb, in one of the parking bays. It protruded from the road paving.

She walked across and knelt down beside it. She thought it might be a tulip. Its head had the gentle cupped shape of a tulip.

But it seemed bigger and more substantial somehow. And its colour was strange. Blue but violet, perhaps a deep red, and there were glimpses of gold. The colours seemed to change as she moved her head around. A trick of light, no doubt.

But the strangest thing about the flower was the way it emerged from a hole in the tarred paving. The hole was perfectly sized to allow the stalk to protrude, and perfectly round as if the stalk had expertly drilled its own exit hole.

But the hole was too small for the colourful head. The stalk must have emerged through the hole and then flowered.

But when? Justine was absolutely sure the flower hadn't been there yesterday. Could it have grown to at least a foot high and sprouted a full bloom all in one day?

She shrugged. Not her area of expertise.

She touched the flower, cupping the tulip-like head and turning it towards her. She thought it was likely to be run over if left where it was, so she decided to pull it out and put it in water at home.

She gripped the stalk and pulled at it gently. It felt firmly anchored. She tugged harder but there was no movement. The stalk felt solidly rooted and strong.

Suddenly, Justine felt light-headed. The colours in the petals seemed to shimmer and move around.

She sat down and steadied her breathing. Once the colours had stopped shifting, she reached out to try again. But she stopped before her fingers made contact with the stalk. She suddenly felt that she shouldn't remove it, even if it were possible.

But what to do? If it was just left here, surely it would be damaged in no time.

Somewhere down the road she heard a car's engine. Digby was awakening.

She pulled her phone from her pocket, opened the camera app and centred the flower in the screen, pressing the button to take a picture.

But the picture was blurred and the colours seemed muted, almost non-existent. She told herself it was another trick of light, but she didn't believe herself.

What to do? She raised her phone and flicked through her contacts. Dad. *Pointless.* Mom. *Pointless.* James. *Why have I not deleted him?* Francois. Her boss, the town building inspector. A few numbers for service providers and her contacts were exhausted.

She bit her lip, filled her lungs to steady her breath, then dialed.

When Francois arrived in his pickup she flagged him to park in the bay next to where the flower stood. He was visibly irritated. She avoided his gaze and simply pointed to the flower.

He frowned and bent to examine it. He took pictures and when he looked at them he grunted and looked over to her. She showed him hers, and he frowned more.

He asked her if she had she planted it, and she wanted to reply with scathing sarcasm, but she only crossed her arms tightly around her body and twitched her head, no.

His frown deepening, Francois touched his phone to dial.

~

Arthur Stokes had been elected Mayor of Digby three years ago, a year before Laura had died. This pre-tourism period of early spring was the time he and Laura had loved their town the most.

Shops and restaurants started to open after the long winter hibernation, while the weather warmed enough to invite ambling on the long waterfront. The local inns began to prepare themselves for their summer season visitors. As Mayor he knew the value of tourism, but once the tourists arrived the peace and quiet would be gone.

He sighed as he parked his car behind Francois' pickup. Easing himself out of his car, he cursed at the aches in his knees and lower back. Not for the first time, he wondered if an SUV would be better for him than his low-slung Ford Mustang, but Laura had so loved the dammed Mustang.

He expected Francois to be alone, but saw a girl standing beside him. The girl looked a little familiar and he realized she was the shy one from the municipal office, the one who never made eye contact. He'd never heard her voice.

A flower. He was called out because of a flower. He was poor at controlling his irritation at the best of times.

He grunted at Francois, ignored the girl and made straight for the flower. Without pausing to examine it he took it in his fist and pulled hard to remove it. Nothing happened. He tried again. Nothing.

He turned on the girl. Did she do this? Was this some kind of prank? She withered, crossed her arms around herself and whimpered that she had only found it.

"So we leave it," he said. "If someone rides over it, so what? It's just a flower."

Francois looked abashed, but the girl transformed. She unravelled her shrunken body and stood straight and defiant. "Can't you see that it's special, rare, precious?"

He looked at it more closely. He couldn't quite identify the colour—it was one colour, then another. It was unusual, and he found himself staring at it despite himself.

But he imagined a morning of phone calls complaining about one precious parking bay being unusable. He reached out to pull it again, but he felt suddenly lightheaded. Too much activity early in the morning without breakfast.

The girl positioned herself between him and the flower, unrecognizable as the tightly-wound introvert she had been a few moments ago. She pointed at him and asked, "Do you really want the headline?"

"Headline? What are you talking about?"

"'Digby mayor callously allows destruction of rare species'."

Arthur swallowed heavily. He didn't know how he had lost control of this, but he had.

He barked at Francois to get a horticultural expert and sort this out, quickly. Then he turned and climbed into his car, taking a last look at the flower and the girl before he drove away.

~

Justine decided to skip work. She'd get a ticking off, especially since the mayor would have her in his sights now. But she had a good record so they couldn't do much about one day off. She told Francois before he left, so she was covered anyway.

She stayed with the flower, spending most of her time sitting on the hard paving next to it. Strangely she didn't find it uncomfortable.

People noticed her and began to drift over. They would see the flower and walk around it. They peppered her with questions but she had few answers. Some asked her why she was sitting there and she told them she wasn't sure, except that she felt like she had to.

Everyone tried to take pictures and they all frowned at the images on their screens. Many of them touched the flower. She worried that the frequent contact might damage the flower, but it seemed too robust.

By lunchtime the flower had grown. She was sure it had stood a foot high this morning, but now it reached almost two feet. She had been sitting there all the time but couldn't explain how it had grown so quickly. Still, there was no doubt it was bigger.

The colours seemed, if anything, even more vivid and yet even more confusing. All morning she had tried to focus and identify one dominant colour. But it eluded her.

By now, a few people had begun to sit around the flower with her.

It was late in the day when Francois arrived with a woman in tow. He introduced her as Liz, an expert in plants.

Liz did the usual things. Pictures that failed, touches that felt intrusive, unsuccessful attempt to pull it out. Justine didn't try to stop her. She felt that the flower could handle itself.

Liz asked Justine questions about how she had found it, had she seen any changes.

Eventually she stepped a few feet away and beckoned Francois over. "I need you to understand something. This is beyond rare. It's unique. I've been working with plants in Nova Scotia for thirty years and I've never seen anything like it. I don't know if something like it exists anywhere else in the world. But I can tell you it doesn't exist here."

"So, someone brought it in," Francois suggested, glancing accusingly at Justine.

But Liz only laughed. "Sure," she said, "someone brought in a seed of something that grew overnight, right through a thick layer of tarred paving, making a perfect little entry hole instead of breaking the paving up, grew two feet high overnight and topped itself with a flower of multi-coloured petals like no-one has ever seen before. And by the way, grew so incredibly strong that grown men can't wrench it from the ground. Makes perfect sense."

Francois blushed, which amused Justine.

The next morning Justine skipped her run and made straight for the flower instead. The colours were more muted in the dark, but still crazily unidentifiable.

As the sun rose and its warm light graced the petals, the colours flared and spun as if driven by some internal energy source, and Justine's breathing surged.

Liz found her a little while later and announced that she had persuaded a professor of horticulture in Halifax to come and see the flower. He should be here in the next day or so.

Then the mayor's Mustang pulled up. Arthur looked weary and worried. He had received a call from someone on Queen street, re-porting "another of them funny flower things, but comin' right through the floor of my shop."

By the time the professor arrived, there were seven reported cases of the strange flower. There may have been more, as word was about that this was a rarity and might have value.

Arthur escorted the professor to the site of the first flower. It had reached about four feet high. Arthur felt its growth might be slowing, but he wasn't sure. The head, now almost a foot itself, was spectacular. The colours remained frustratingly impossible to grasp and identify, a moving kaleidoscope of vivid primary and secondary colours.

There was a permanent encampment around that first flower now, Justine at its centre. She was speaking to the gathering frequently, gesturing while they sat around her in apparent reverence.

Arthur watched her intently as he walked across the road with the professor. She seemed to reach an end to whatever she was saying and held her arms above her head with the hands closing towards each other, a crude imitation of the flower's tulip shape.

A sermon, Arthur thought, *she was delivering a sermon.*

Then, astonishingly, the crowd around her rose from their sitting positions and made the same gesture.

As he was leaving, the professor fumbled with his car remote, pressing the wrong button and setting off an alarm that took him a few seconds to cancel. He was trembling slightly and ran his hand through his hair compulsively.

Before he entered his car he turned to Arthur. "I have a PhD," he announced. "Do you know that puts me in less than two percent of the world's population? I'm an expert. A *bona fide* expert, you understand?" Arthur nodded, but not sure why.

"Do you know how often people like me discover something genuinely, unequivocally new?" the professor challenged him.

Arthur shrugged. "I have no idea."

"Genuinely new discoveries are rare, more rare than you can imagine. Only a tiny fraction of the most learned people in the world get to find something that hasn't even been hinted at or even imagined."

He took a deep breath. "That's what you have here. You don't have any idea yet how this will explode. But be wise. Prepare."

Over the next two days the numbers of reported flowers grew to more than thirty. They appeared in roads and in patches of grass; they came through the floors of buildings. Each time they were found in the early morning.

Devotees began patrolling the streets throughout the night, desperately hoping to sight a flower emerging.

Media vans arrived. They made the usual futile attempts to film the flowers. One group brought along an artist to sketch them, but everyone who saw the finished work disagreed on the artist's choice of colours.

Arthur was standing at the gas pump when he saw a pickup turn in, packed high with household goods and with a family stuffed into the cabin. Andy Turner climbed out and looked abashed when he saw Arthur standing there.

"Family can't take it anymore, Arthur. Can't sleep at night, wondering if one of them things will invade our house. Kids are scared all the time. No-one knows what they are or what they're about." He sighed. "Just gotta get out."

The Turners may or may not have been the first to leave, but they were far from the last. The roads were busy, on one side with cars and trucks taking people away, on the other side with journalists, students, academics and the plain curious coming in.

Most of these were day-trippers, but a new kind of visitor began to emerge. They always asked for Justine. They wore t-shirts that were dyed in multiple colours, printed with an image of a tulip-like plant on a stalk in relief. Arthur thought it looked like a champagne flute. Others were printed with a stylized outline of a girl holding her arms above her head with the hands close together.

The flower began to be known as Digby's Grace, but some insisted on calling it The Lady Justine.

In coffee shops and check-out tills, the girl and the flowers were the only topic of conversation. At the Sea Biscuit one morning, Arthur overheard a conversation between two women.

"And the thing is, Justine *is* a virgin after all. That means something, don't it?" said one of the women.

Arthur looked them over, knowing that neither of them were from the town and that they knew nothing about the girl.

After three weeks there were few locals left. A trickle of people from out of town became a stream that grew into a river. A growing number of houses were closing up and parts of the town took on a derelict look.

The grifters had held on to the end, trying to squeeze every advantage possible. They'd made some money from the tourists, but the growing influx of devotees were poor marks. They didn't want cheap selfies with a strangely blurred shadow form as mementos. They wanted the experience. They headed straight for the site of the first flower and looked for Justine.

Eventually even the grifters gave up on their broken town and its fanatical invaders.

Arthur held on. He thought of leaving but couldn't. It wasn't duty, loyalty or fondness for the place that held him. This town, for all its flaws and for all its current madness, was the only thing keeping him from utter loneliness.

He stopped his Mustang a little way down Water Street, across from the first flower. Now there was a shrine. A tall wooden structure, shaped in that now-familiar flute shape on a tall stem.

There was a step in front of the structure and Justine stood upon it, her arms spread, hair loose, smiling at the throng of people kneeling in front of her. She wore a loose robe emblazoned with the chaotic colours. She spoke something and the crowd chanted back. A practised chant.

Arthur drove to the end of Water Street, weaving slowly to avoid flowers and the congregations of people surrounding them. Shrines were being erected at different spots, most took the shape of the flute, but some were carved reliefs of a girl with head bent and arms raised with fingertips touching above her head.

He drove past the closed shops and the abandoned homes. He felt weary. *What would Laura have made of this?*

And then he realized that he couldn't recall her face. He stopped his car in the middle of the road and began to weep.

He turned off the car engine, opened the door, and walked towards the flower closest to him. He knelt.

~

In the space of just two nights, the flowers were all gone. They died as quickly as they had appeared. The bulbs of many colours turned grey and fell to the ground, where they quickly decayed into a slimy mush. The stalks shrank and disappeared beneath the holes they had made.

The academics scrambled to retrieve samples of living tissue they could study, but what the samples revealed, no one knew, for the analysis was never shared publicly.

The scientists, academics, students and tourists waited for a little while, but when there was no sign of the flowers reappearing, they left quickly.

The devotees waited longer. They waited for something, but eventually gave in to the dull reality that it was over.

The two devotee factions grew edgy with each other. Each blamed the other for the disappearance of the flowers. Words were exchanged and insults hurled. On one occasion stones were thrown.

After another few days even their enmity lost its passion and they began to drift away. Some of the statues were loaded up and taken with them, others were left to join the mess that was Digby.

~

Arthur walked with Justine through their town together. "Hard to believe what it was just a week ago," he said.

She didn't respond right away. She had a confident air, holding her head up and looking around with interest.

She turned to face him. Her eyes held his. Her arms were held behind her back with her hands clasped, instead of being wrapped around her. "They will come back," she said suddenly.

"The flowers?"

She smiled. "The people. The people will come back."

"Hmph," he responded. "You know the municipality is down to just you and me?"

She nodded.

"Well, shall we get to work?"

This is the New World

My arms are held tightly, painfully. One of the men pulls me, the other prefers to push me, so I struggle to keep balance. My feet drag at times and that makes them both more impatient, so they push/pull me even more.

I stumble and would fall, but they yank hard at me so that my arms feel like they are being ripped out of their sockets. I want to cry out, but they have bound a scarf over my mouth. I have to force my breathing, ragged and sore. If I did cry out, it might make me choke and I don't think I can control that.

We reach stairs that make it worse. The stairwell is narrow and cannot fit the three of us together, so the puller moves ahead and the pusher moves behind, and I'm propelled between them so that I cannot place my feet.

I fall and my knee cracks against the edge of the uncarpeted stairs. I'm dragged up, and I fall again and this time it is my hip. Again I am dragged up, and again I fall, and my rib cage smacks into the stairs right where I am bruised from where the tall one punched me earlier.

Then, finally, we reach the top of the stairs. I try to balance and calm my breathing, but it's hopeless.

The shorter one knocks on a door, politely, which surprises me given their roughness so far.

A muffled voice calls back.

The two men manhandle me upright so they can both stand at

attention. There are more excruciating moments of discomfort and pain before the door finally opens.

Whoever opens the door moves to the side with it, and my captors push me hard into the gap. I cannot help but fall, but my feet move instinctively to try and keep me upright and I perform an awkward off-balance crawl that takes me skidding rapidly across the room.

My head crashes into a solid wooden desk. A bolt of pain slashes through my brain, my eyes burn and fill with tears. My head feels like it is rolling aimlessly like one of those silly wobble toys people used to put on dashboards. I try to stand but my legs give way and I collapse to the floor.

I hear voices a distance away, but somehow I know they are close by. Sounds and images swim slowly around me, strangely out of sync with each other. I make an effort to take control of my head movements and focus on my breathing.

The whirl of images and sounds slows and snatches of conversation begin to slip into order.

"....trying to walk in on the 217."

"Just like that, walking down the 217?" It was a woman's voice.

"Just like that."

"The 217, not the 101."

"Like I said, 217."

"Interesting. So he knew to turn off the 101 some way back."

"Yep, figure he knows the area a bit."

"Or a lot. Was he alone?"

"Just him. Might have had a van though."

"Might have?"

"We moved a bit down the 217 to see if there was anyone else. Saw a van in the trees, a way aways, but it coulda been one of those abandoned ones from before. It was getting kinda dark an' all."

"Jesus, Tim. You know better than that. Get someone back out there now. Check it out."

The man Tim tries to protest but he's cut off quickly and I hear the door opening and closing again.

As my sight regains focus I look around. The office seems large enough. Space for the large desk, a couple of chairs in front of it, and a small coffee table in the corner with another four armchairs astride it. An executive office.

There are posters on the wall behind the desk, fixed crudely with Sellotape. One has the letters DSZ superimposed over a coat of arms made of a machine gun and a syringe crossed over each other. Another is in the style of the old Soviet propaganda images, with heroic figures surrounded by admiring crowds. These heroes are medical staff armed with syringes, and workers armed with guns. All are masked. Those posters proclaim DSZ at the top, and at the footer of each are the slogans, "Together Strong, Together Safe."

One more poster shows a thick chain wrapped protectively around and around a town, with what appear to be zombies flailing vainly against the chain wall. Some of the zombies hold signs saying "no vaccines," or, "no masks." The poster's slogan, scrawled at the bottom, is, "They won't break *our* chain. No weak links."

"Hey."

A woman is standing over me. She is dressed in denim jeans, well-worn by the look of them, but none of those false rips that were fashionable when fashion mattered. She wears a light blue golf shirt stretched over her ample midriff and bulging arms. The golf shirt has the DSZ logo on its left breast. Her hair is flecked with grey and pulled back tightly into a severe ponytail. Armed with a gun, she would look like one of the heroes on the poster.

Before I can talk, the door opens and shuts again. I hear Tim's voice. "Sent Donny. Annie will go with him, so he's not alone out there."

"Okay, thanks, Tim." The woman's is calmer now. She bends over and peers into my eyes. "He's coming around. Get him in the chair."

I am rough handled by two men again. The second guy must have stayed quietly in the background while Tim spoke to the woman.

"Jesus, guys," she snaps, "take it easy. We need to ask him questions. Can you try to preserve him enough to do that?"

The men ease off and get me settled into a chair without further pain. Then my arms are pulled back and something is whipped around my wrists behind the chair back.

"Wait outside," she tells Tim and his mate.

"What's your name?" she asks. She leans against the front of the desk, standing above me rather than sitting on the other side of it.

I am still sore and barely conscious. I don't respond.

She raises an eyebrow, and repeats the question with emphasis.

I swallow hard, and say, "Martin. Martin Kimble."

She nods. "Good. I'm Abigail. And where you from, Martin?"

"Does it matter?"

She stares at me intently for a moment, then, "Listen good now. There's a strong likelihood this night will go badly for you, and attitude pretty much guarantees it. So my advice is to you is this. Try not to give me the impression you're a man with something to hide, how's that sound?"

I nod.

"Where you from, Martin Kimble?"

I hesitate, then, "North Carolina."

"Jesus." She whispers. "Jesus." She backs away, retreating behind the large desk. She checks her mask, self consciously tightening it around her nose and mouth. "Wait," she says with suspicion, "You don't sound like North Carolina. You could be from around here."

I shrug. "Work," I mumble. "Had to move there a few years ago."

"North effin' Carolina. Are you kidding me?"

I shake my head. There is a long pause.

"Am I under arrest?" I ask.

"Under arrest? Are you serious? You're a walking dead, and you shuffle your way into our safe zone. You think you have rights here? North Carolina, for god's sake. Hell, arrest would be a favour." She snorts.

I shrug again.

"Whereabouts around here? I don't recall a Martin Kimble."

"Kentville."

"Kentville. Shit. Did you have family there?"

"Got my wife and daughter out. That's what matters."

"Good job." She says, with a hint of compassion.

Kentville had been a popular town with an affluent population of mostly retired people, right in the heart of the beautiful Annapolis Valley. Like most of Nova Scotia, the town had sailed through COVID with little discomfort, and prospered during the phony years when it seemed the pandemic was over.

When the Tampa variant emerged and slaughtered half a million people in a month, the world went crazy. Florida's politicians dithered over lockdowns so the federal government sent troops and closed off its borders. It was too late. Tampa got out and mutated further into the deadly Atlanta and Houston variants.

"Still don't know how Houston got into Kentville." Abigail is musing now.

I stare at her blankly.

"Wasn't an issue for you then, was it?"

She pulls her shoulders back and her face tightens. "We made the right call."

"Yep." I nod. "The world-famous Republic of Digby."

"We never called it that. Just the Digby Safe Zone."

"Still, you locked us all out."

"Had to. No way to beat Houston once it gets in."

I said nothing.

She stared at me for a while, then, "How'd you end up in North Carolina, of all places?"

I grimace. "Tried here, of course. But no way in. You made sure of that."

"No apologies. We could see what was happening. We had a couple of deniers making noises, but we got rid of them quickly. What we did, it was hard, but it saved our lives."

I grunted. "Lot of folks like me would have been supporters. But you kept us out."

"Like I said, no apologies. So we didn't let you in. We're bad people, blah, blah, blah. Still doesn't answer my question. North Carolina?"

"Deniers. Once we hit a brick wall here we wandered around, trying to find anyone who would take us in. Tried hitching for rides but no one was picking up anyone. We were tired and so damn hungry. Then a van pulls up and offers us a ride."

"Deniers," Abigail said.

"Didn't know that right away. They checked our temperatures and gave us a lift. Couple of other people in there. They had a bit of food and water. They were nice. We felt like we'd lucked out. When we stopped at night to camp they talked about how we need to stick together. Told us there's folks who are beating the virus."

"You believed them?"

"When you've watched your wife and little girl starve and bleed through their shoes for three days and someone comes along and offers you kindness and hope, you'll believe a lot. Besides, they never talked about masks or vaccines or any of that stuff. Just said there's a place where things are better. I wanted to believe it and I did." I glared up at her defiantly but she seemed satisfied.

"Still a long way from here to North Carolina."

I shrug again. I don't feel much like explaining the long and meandering journey that led us to our rescuers' promised land. "It was a long trip but that's where they were heading," was all I offered.

"And now you're hoping for asylum after you've seen the fuck up they've made?"

Abandoning the safety of the desk between us, she walks around it to me. She's studying me as if I'm an exhibit. She stops in front of me and leans back against the desk. She swings her arm and smacks me hard across my face.

She is strong, the smack stings and my eyes tear up. I feel nausea rising.

"In case you think that's me starting to beat a story out of you, it ain't. I got more effective people for that. It was just a quick reminder that I ain't a fool and I won't be taken for one. Okay?"

She is very calm despite the violent act. I nod my agreement.

"You don't add up, Martin Kimble. My guys caught you on the 217," she continues, "but why would you be right on the road like that? Anyone trying to sneak in would have tried harder not to be seen. Besides, anyone who knows about our Safe Zone, and you do, would know there's no walk-in asylum here. Lockout is lockout. And now, you're sitting here facing execution and you're just as calm as a monk. Then there's the big question. If you're here to join our virus-free safety zone, where's that wife and kid?"

I can't help but tear up. I turn my face down but she's seen, and she grabs my chin and forces me to look at her.

"Dammit Kimble, you better tell me what's going on. Where is your family?"

I take a deep breath, turn my eyes to hers and she sees the pain in mine. She drops her hand and backs away.

I swallow hard. "They were everything, Jen and Carrie. Moving to a new city isn't easy, and it makes you closer. Then you find you're surrounded by deniers, and you feel isolated. You cling to each other."

I pause to compose myself. "Jen got it and she died." My voice catches. "Now it's just me and Carrie."

Despite myself, I choke. I can't help but cough, and Abigail backs away quickly.

"Now she has it, my Carrie." My voice cracks and I'm sobbing. "She's all I have, she's my life. And they have her, you understand?"

She nods, but I say, "No you don't. There's nothing but shit and more shit down there. The Patriots run everything. Protecting our freedoms, they say. But it's a dictatorship and everything we had is gone. No hospitals operating. No equipment, no medicines, not unless you're one of them. People get the virus and they just die at home. If they have a home. Most places are commandeered now, by the Patriots. And Carrie, she's—"

"Wait," she commands. "I want to hear more."

She moves to the door and I hear her call, "Get Joy here. I want him tested, like now."

She turns to me. "I gotta leave you here until you're tested. We'll continue after."

I wait for maybe ten or fifteen minutes. Digby isn't a large place so finding the person called Joy can't be too hard.

Then the door opens again and a woman bustles in. She's dressed head to toe in protective clothing, masks, latex gloves and safety glasses. She examines me quickly and efficiently. She takes her sample and runs it through the test with a routine efficiency.

"He's okay," she declares. "No symptoms, test is clean."

"He could be carrying though?" Abigail asks anxiously.

Joy shrugs. "Just gotta keep a close watch on him. Call me if any symptoms show."

Joy leaves. I see the one called Tim let her out the door, which he closes after her. He looks unconvinced and angry.

Abigail is thoughtful, and as close to an ally as I can get. She stands in front of me again. "You're shitting me, Kimble."

"What do you mean?"

"I figure you're a guy who landed up in anti-vaxxer hell. Your wife dies, that's tough. You hate the place, you hate them. Then the thing you love most is taken hostage by the Patriots. They can treat her or not, depending on what you do. Have I got it right so far?"

I nod.

"You're not here because you ran away. You're here because they sent you."

I tilt my head to acknowledge she's right.

"So, what do they want from you? You're a Nova Scotian boy, you know Digby. They must have picked you for that. Local knowledge. But why? What do they gain by sending you here?"

She waits and I say nothing. I wait for another slap, but it doesn't come.

"Maybe you're here to spy. Tell them what we're up to. But it doesn't make sense, you know? You'd make a pretty awful spy. You're an emotional wreck and you're not exactly James Bond. Walking down the 217 like it's a summer stroll. And what can you tell them they don't already know? Pretty much it's them on one side, us on the other. Not much to tell."

I continue to hold my silence. I can see she's finding her way.

"So I figure they want something bad. So bad they'd hold a little girl hostage for it. They claim to be Christian folk down there, so taking a little girl hostage ain't a small thing, even for them."

She peers at me again, for an uncomfortable time. I adjust myself to try and ease the pressure on my bruises, but it's a vain effort.

"She was lovely, was Jen," I say at last. "Not your fashion model type, but she had a shine that came from way inside her. People liked her. She was sweet. She never even argued with the deniers. Just smiled at them and changed the subject. Even they were drawn to her."

Abigail frowns and Tim looks impatient. I strain my neck to find the other guy. He is squatting on the floor, looking bored.

"Now Carrie, she's more like me. Takes life more seriously. She hates it there. Hates being surrounded by them. Wishes we'd never left here."

Tim looks at Abigail and she nods. "You're stalling."

I take a breath. "Now Cathy, Cathy's something else. Cathy's a firecracker."

Abigail and Tim look at each other, puzzled.

"She's a true believer, that one. Doesn't matter how bad it gets there, it's like she doesn't see what's right in front of her. She truly believes all the conspiracy bullshit. Cathy's a classic patriot, believes the virus is bullshit and the cure is the real enemy."

"What the hell you talking about?" demands Tim. "Who's Cathy?"

Right now, there's a knock at the door. Tim goes to answer. He talks briefly to someone and comes back looking worried. "That van, it ain't there no more."

"Now," I say as if there had been no interruption, "Cathy's beautiful. No, that's not right. She's more than beautiful. Cathy's sexy. Red hot, smoking, sexy. Especially in weather like this when she can wear her thin little strap top with no bra. And with those boobs. Oh my. Cathy's so good looking, even the virus figured it couldn't take her out of this world, so it made her a carrier instead. Houston doesn't take her out, but it sure likes to be carried by her."

Their impatience is gone. In its place is a look of creeping fear.

"You can just see it, can't you?" I continue, "Cathy walks into a bar filled with a bunch of guys sitting around drinking, no masks. She walks in, bright and perky with her million-dollar smile and that cleavage showing. 'Hi, y'all,' she'll call. 'Hi, y'all.'" I put emphasis on the breathy H. "Hi, y'all."

"Oh shit." Abigail exclaims.

Tim rushes out. His mate unfolds himself from the floor and lumbers after him.

"You're a decoy," Abigail states, her eyes wide with shock and fear.

"I didn't have a choice. I'll tell you which bar, you can track who was there tonight. But it won't make any difference. It's already spreading."

"But you, you rode with her. We tested you...."

"They pumped me full of boosters before we set off. Supposed to slow it long enough."

She looks skeptical.

"Oh, you think they don't have vaccines down there? You think the boys in charge don't look after themselves?" I snort in derision. "You could test me again tomorrow and it would show. But you won't bother, will you?"

"They sent you on a suicide mission."

"Either way." I acknowledge.

"Why?" she asks.

"Cause Carrie gets treatment if I do it."

"Shit. But why do they want this? What's their gain? Do they hate us so much?"

I laugh. It's a short and ragged laugh that devolves into a cough. I stare at her. "You can't be allowed to win. Don't you see? The worse things get down there, the more they double down the lies. And it works, mostly. But the rumours keep coming, about this place where everyone's vaccinated and the virus is beaten. You're winning, and they can't allow it."

"They'll kill us, just to protect a lie that's already killing them?"

"You think it's about life and death. Not for the Patriots. It's all power. Who wins, who loses," is all I say.

I'm bundled out in the dark early hours. There'll be no trial, no public hearing for me. My story has to be hidden.

Abigail has summoned others, I presume her DSZ committee. They stop their discussions to glare at me as I am dragged out. There is anger in their eyes, but I think I see a hint of compassion in Abigail's.

"I love you Carrie. Be Better," are my last thoughts before I'm forced onto the boat that will take my body out to sea.

Wise Man

My office is an overgrown closet. A wooden desk, very old, stained and pitted. An orthopaedic chair, very new, an indulgence. Two cheap wooden spindle chairs between the desk and the door. Their legs are in need of strengthening. Thankfully, they are rarely used. Grey metal filing cabinets, piled atop with stacks of old editions, line up against the one wall.

There is a window on the wall opposite the filing cabinets, but it's covered by a large, framed map of Digby and its surrounds. The office door is set in one of those old English industrial-style panels of dark wood and textured glass windows that provide partial privacy from sight but none from sound. I think the fluorescent light in the ceiling is considered an unhealthy choice these days, but, well, I need light.

Beyond the door is a slightly larger office with desks for my two part-time employees.

It is a functional space that serves its limited purpose. Here I write the town's gossip once a week (carefully edited so as not to cause offence), lay out official notices, take an occasional phone call and type up ads for the smalls page.

Publishing a small weekly newspaper leaves many idle moments. In those moments, I indulge my fantasy to be an author of actual literature, printed in a book, sold in bookstores.

My cramped and sterile office is very effective at sucking the life out of those wasteful ideas.

I don't dislike my office space. But at times I need to escape it.

A year ago the town buzzed with talk about a new, upmarket coffee shop opening on Water Street. Conventional wisdom around town talked down its prospects. Digby is a working-class town. The word 'upmarket' tends to provoke derision rather than support.

"Why would anyone pay four dollars for a coffee when you can get one at Timmy's for two?" was the typical retort, long before anyone had seen a menu or price list.

But from the day she opened, Dorothy proved her doubters wrong. Digby Roaster is a cut above anything else in town and continues to flourish to this day with a loyal clientele, myself included.

I wandered in the morning they opened, curious, and hopeful, too. Ah, the aroma of fresh ground coffee instead of the bitter smell of yesterday's reheated leftovers. That alone was a reason to fall in love with the place. But there was more.

Under the counter on the side wall was a glass display filled with tempting cheesecakes topped with berries or jellies, fat and puffy biscuits, croissants and a variety of small cakes. Far too much cream for my taste, but a feast for the eyes, and my mouth watered.

A blackboard stretched the length of the wall behind the counter, with menus for drinks, snacks and a daily special written playfully in different-coloured chalks. The lighting was soft, respecting the natural light that flowed in from the front wall of glass.

I ran my fingers on the surface of a table and smiled at the comforting touch of real wood.

I found a table in the corner and took my laptop from my backpack. I was digging around for my headphones when I heard a voice that was still familiar, though it came from long ago.

"Hi. How's your day so far?" She asked.

I looked up at her. It was the tail end of COVID, so she wore a face mask, but her eyes were unmistakable.

I hesitated. *Say hi. No, just be the customer. Say hi.* "Hi....Shannon?" I swallowed hard.

She frowned for a moment then her eyes lit up and she said, "Oh, my god, Harold."

Her excitement sounded genuine, and I flushed and nodded. We chatted for a moment, exchanging pointless observations about how many years it had been, and how me and Billy and Luke had always been such goofy guys in high school. That made me smile inside, because we had all three been shy introverts. But making Shannon laugh had been our narcotic. Billy once said Shannon laughed like a happy song tapped out on crystal plates.

She asked me what I wanted. *She means from the menu, Harold,* and I asked for a biscuit, thinking as she walked away that I would suffer terribly for the cream.

She returned shortly with the biscuit and it was indeed loaded with cream. I took a fork full and smiled and she beamed back at me.

"Good, ain't it?"

I nodded enthusiastically.

She made a little gesture suggesting she needed to see to other customers, but I didn't want to lose her beam yet, so I dared to inquire about Tom.

Her eyes dimmed but she managed a tight smile and told me they were no longer together. I lied that I was sorry. But I was flustered and I said I didn't want to keep her from her other customers.

Tom and Shannon had been the cliché golden couple. So beautiful, so popular, so destined. Being around them was like bathing in a beautiful promise. *But you showered in hurt as well. Because you were just one of those goofy guys.*

Shannon went to attend to other people. I put on my headphones, intending to listen to soft music while I caught up on emails and worked my way through the coffee and biscuit. The emails didn't take long, but I found words began to float around my head, I opened a blank document and started to type.

Digby Roaster became my regular refuge. I wrote something each time I was there. I had no illusions about my writing, but I was pleased enough that I wrote at anything all. The ambience encouraged me. The roaster was so *not* my office.

But it wasn't just the roaster and its inviting décor. There was something I couldn't quite describe. Something about being surrounded by strangers yet being alone. It gave me a curious feeling of simultaneous connection and detachment that tugged my brain just a little bit out of its predictable routines.

And of course, there was Shannon.

I didn't raise the subject of Tom again. But Digby is a small town with small town gossips, and it wasn't difficult to learn some things from a few subtle inquiries.

Tom had lurched from one cliché to another, the once envied and always-popular high school jock who becomes the good old boy spending nights out with friends who share a love of drink and all the troubles it attracts. Work neither interested nor motivated him.

When Shannon gave birth to Amy, she moved into his parents' house, where she was treated well as a daughter but evidently not well as a wife. It was in their fourth year that she called time.

When the divorce came through, Tom took off on a motorcycle to ride across Canada and find himself. It was said that he had made it no further than the other side of the ferry to New Brunswick, where he now worked in a bar and was rumoured to be involved with the bar's owner.

I visit the Roaster two or three times a week. Most days it's Shannon who welcomes me and points me to the small table near the back, the one I prefer, where I can observe but stay barely noticed.

Each time she says hello I feel like she makes that smile just for me. But I watch her greeting others and I think they all must feel the same.

One day I was engrossed in a poem I was attempting to write. I'm not fond of poetry, but I was taking an online writing course and was working on one of the exercises.

A shadow fell. I glanced up and realized the shadow was created by a man who stood in the door. From head to toes and shoulder to shoulder he filled the opening, with scattered slices of light outlining him.

I knew many people in Digby but no one of that bulk. I squinted to see him more clearly. He had on a cap that may once have been a ten-gallon cowboy hat but had softened and flopped around the edges. He wore a long woollen coat despite the fine weather outdoors. It may have been grey but may also have been a faded brown. The coat was held around the waist by a dirty rope tied in a simple bow knot like you would use on a shoe.

He stepped forward, allowing the door to close behind him, and removed his hat as men used to do a time ago. As he stepped forward the light was allowed back in, revealing fraying on the hem and sleeves of his coat. His hair and beard were long and appeared untended. On his feet were a pair of very old and worn trainers. The soles looked so thin it must be painful to walk in them.

He glanced around nervously at the few seated customers. Conversation had died. Every pair of eyes was turned to him.

Then Shannon walked out of the kitchen. Without hesitation she greeted him with her usual brightness and guided him over to a table. She asked if he wanted coffee or tea, and maybe something to eat?

He mumbled and, reaching into one of the coat pockets, took out a coin that he offered to her, but she waved her hand and said, "Oh, tush! On the house."

When she went back to the kitchen he sat with his arms resting on the table top, his hands clasped. Most customers had bent their heads, but their attention was still on him and the shop was eerily quiet. The man kept his eyes focused on his clasped hands.

When Shannon returned to him with coffee and a sandwich, he held his hands together in front of his face in a gesture of thanks. He looked directly into her eyes for a moment, then smiled.

As he turned to his food and drink, for a tiny moment his gaze passed over to me and he caught me staring. I thought I noticed a very slight nod, but I may have been mistaken.

He consumed slowly, and the coffee shop returned to its usual low buzz of conversation, his presence no longer distracting. I tapped at my laptop again, but I was intrigued, and I glanced up at him frequently.

Every now and then I would see him busy with something on his table. It looked like he was writing with great concentration.

When Shannon returned to clear up his plate and mug, he gave her that penetrating look again and I saw his hand lift and take hold of hers. He released her hand and she turned away, but she looked at something in her hand as she did. She passed my table on her way back to the counter and I caught a glimpse of her. Her eyes were wide and her face was flushed.

The man reached into his pocket and pulled out a very worn paperback, which he proceeded to read, ignoring the continued glances from those around him.

Shannon came back to my table to see if I needed anything.

As she was about to go I called, "Shannon."

She turned and tilted her head quizzically.

"Is everything okay? Did that guy upset you?"

"No!" Her brow furrowed. "He's a sweet guy."

"I'm sorry I didn't mean....it's just that you seemed upset when you walked away. And he's not from around here"

"You mean he's homeless," she said and I felt disapproved of.

"I didn't mean....I just was concerned, that's all."

Her eyes softened and she said, "it's okay, I know you mean well. You always do."

I felt my breath tighten a little as she said that.

"It's just he gave me a note, that's all."

"Can I ask what he wrote?"

She hesitated, then took a small scrap of paper from her apron pocket. The writing on it was tiny, scratchy and hard to read. I squinted and read, "There is pain in loneliness, but worse pain is being with someone who makes you feel alone."

I saw tears well up in the corners of Shannon's eyes. She hurriedly excused herself and scurried back to the kitchen.

I glanced over to where the man sat, and he was staring at me. There was no aggression in his gaze, nor even curiosity. It was as if he simply recognized my presence.

I packed up and left shortly after. I glanced at him as I passed him and he glanced back, nodding his head softly as he did.

I was next at the Roaster two days later. As I walked in Shannon's eyes flashed me her brightest smile and she pointed me to my favourite table. She didn't bother to ask me if I wanted coffee.

But before I moved from the entrance, I heard a soft cough at my side. The man was sitting there again. He nodded to me. I nodded back.

Sitting across the table from him was Davie. Davie did occasional repair work for me. I had known him from high school. Despite only being one year behind me at school, he had taken to calling me Mister Harold. Despite my frequent protestations he had continued to do so ever since.

"Hey, Mister Harold, how you doing? This here is John." He pointed to the homeless man.

"Nice to see you Davie. Good to meet you, John"

He nodded again and smiled. I made my way to my table.

When Shannon brought me my coffee she asked if I wanted a biscuit today and I said, perhaps just a muffin. I hadn't found a way to tell her I didn't like cream and I couldn't correct her when she occasionally just put down a cream-loaded biscuit without asking.

I was halfway through my coffee and muffin, contemplating my laptop, when Davie wandered over. John was heading out the door, waving to Shannon as he left.

"Hey, Mister Harold."

"Hey, Davie." I gestured for him to sit.

He did so and leaned in towards me as if conspirators. "Interesting guy, that." He indicated the table where John had sat with his thumb.

I asked him why, and he said, "Mister Harold, you know how I get a bit down now and then?"

"Of course."

Davie was a cordial and likeable man. But he was prone to occasional bouts of despair. A poor scholar, he had left school early to work in his father's repair business, which paid him little for a lot of dirty work. He desperately wanted more for his three children and had tried his hand at many side business ventures. His effort couldn't be faulted, but success had eluded him. He took each setback hard.

"I don't know how he could've known me. I can't recall what I must have said to him, Mister Harold, and he don't talk back, do you know? I can't think I told him much at all, and its not like I talked for long, you know?"

I must have looked puzzled, for he scratched in his pocket and brought out another small torn-off scrap of paper with something written in tiny script. *Going down happens. Don't worry. Staying down is the only failure.*

I frowned. Then I realized Shannon was hovering, following our conversation. I held up the paper and raised an eyebrow to Davie, looking to Shannon. Davie nodded, and I passed the note to her.

She read it and nodded like it confirmed something she knew. "Did you hear what he wrote for Angie?" she asked. "*Losing life brings grief. Remaking your life brings recovery.*'" She shook her head. "How could he know that Angie was struggling so much since Ben died?"

"Wow," Davie drawled, his jaw hanging open.

Shannon went on to claim that Angie had cried when she took the note, but from the next day she had seemed stronger, more positive.

"Hey Mister Harold, you should write about John in your paper," Davie said suddenly.

"Write what?"

"He's got some kind of powers Mister Harold, don't you see? He's like one of them seven garlies."

"Svengali? They're usually evil, Davie."

"Oh, well, then he's like a good version of them."

"Actually," Shannon chimed in, "Davie's got a point. You know what its like in a small town like this? Word gets around. Already there's people come in here asking about the spooky homeless guy. People will start making their own stories about him and they could be bad stories. You won't do that Harold: you're a good man. You'll do his story fair and honest."

I flushed when she said that, and I wondered if she saw the colour in my cheeks.

I couldn't think what I would write about a strange homeless man writing pithy wisdoms to random people, and my little newspaper wasn't into sensation and intrigue. But I offered a compromise. I would sit with John and talk to him myself. Then I would decide if there was something to write.

I returned the following morning and Shannon right away signalled that John was in the washroom. I saw his plate and mug at his usual table, so I took the seat opposite his.

In a few minutes I felt his shadow move past me. He nodded as he took his seat, gesturing with his hands as if offering me the seat I had already taken.

"Morning, do you mind if I sit?"

He chuckled slightly and doffed his head in acknowledgement. "I run the local newspaper."

Yes, his nod confirmed. I didn't think it mattered how he knew that. "There are some who think I should write about you."

If I expected him to be shocked or concerned, I was wrong. He only smiled and shrugged. *Flattered but humble*, I read in his body language.

"Perhaps I can ask you a few questions?" I took out my notepad and pen, placing them on the table in front of me.

He opened his hands in a welcoming gesture and leaned back in his chair.

I coughed lightly to ready myself. For a small local paper like the *Echo* I was rarely called upon to interview someone and I found myself a little unready.

"Where you are from?" Seemed like an easy beginning.

He frowned and thought for a moment. The he turned to the window and gestured with a motion that captured everything outside.

"From away, I know. But where specifically?"

He pointed to my notebook and raised his eyebrows at me. I picked it up and handed it to him, with the pen. He quickly drew a rough impression of Canada, marking an X on the west coast.

"Vancouver?"

He nodded enthusiastically.

I raised my eyebrows. "That's a long journey."

He only shrugged. Then he leaned forward, resting his elbows on the table. I shrank back as his unwashed odour drifted over me. Then I realized the odour was mild and inoffensive. I had reacted to my expectations, and I felt embarrassed.

I coughed to hide my embarrassment. "You have a habit of giving people words of wisdom."

He nodded again, tilting his head a little.

I paused for a moment. "What you wrote for Shannon. It closely resembles something Robin William said once." I waited for a reaction but there was none, so I continued. "What you wrote for Davie. That's Muhammad Ali. And for Angie, Anne Riophe."

To my surprise he grinned. Then he pointed at me, then at his head, then me again. I think he was telling me I was clever.

He held a hand up as if telling me to wait, then he busied himself in his pockets. I realized the large coat had deep pockets on the outside and inside. After a moment he brandished a battered book. It was Dickens' *A Tale of Two Cities*. He placed it on the table.

From another pocket emerged an equally worn book, *On the Road* by Jack Kerouac. That seemed appropriate.

Then one which, although small enough to fit in his pocket, was entitled *The Big Book of Quotes*.

Continuing, he emptied his pockets, placing alongside the books a few coins, a pair of reading glasses, a pair of very worn gloves, a half-empty bottle of water and his well-used notepad and pen. He spread his hands over the display.

"These are all your possessions?" I asked.

He nodded.

No phone.

I raised an eyebrow. "You have no connection to"—I gestured with my hands—"the world out there."

He grinned at that, then shook his head and picked up the three books, shaking them in front of me.

"These are not connections. They are entertainment."

He smiled quite gently and offered an open-handed shrug that said it mattered not.

I waited. My job wasn't one that honed interviewing skills, but I remembered enough training to know there are times when it is best to leave an awkward pause that most people cannot resist talking to fill.

John did not. He leaned back with his hands relaxed in his lap and returned my gaze. I think this standoff lasted a minute. But a minute of silent awkwardness can seem like an hour.

It was I who spoke to fill the void. "I just want to understand, John. People seem to appreciate your advice, but if they know it comes from a book, what will they think?"

He smiled at me again, a tolerant smile like one given to a child who means well but doesn't understand. I flushed.

He tore another strip from his notepad. I resolved to buy him a pack of notepads before he left Digby. On his scrap he scratched, *what, or why?*

I frowned. "I don't understand."

He stared with eyes that penetrated me so I felt exposed, and I couldn't understand why.

What, or why?

I read the words over and over, my frown deepening. I felt foolish, inadequate. Then it dawned on me.

"You don't think it's what you say to people that's important. Its *why* you think they need it said."

He beamed at me, reached over and shook my hand. I didn't pull back.

I felt as if I had the shape of a thing but couldn't name it. My frown deepened as I struggled to understand what John was and what he was doing with people in Digby. He gazed at me with eyes soft and face relaxed. I felt very warm and comfortable under his gaze.

He reached for his pad again, this time tearing a strip slowly. The pace of his actions seemed to have their own language. This gesture spoke to me of reassurance.

I tapped on the table top, unsure how to respond. Then Shannon appeared to ask if we needed anything. We both declined and she moved away.

He nodded towards her.

"What?" I tried for casual but I'm sure I produced defensive.

Still, he smiled at me with those gentle eyes and I felt like he was softening a sharp edge in me.

"Is it so obvious?"

He gave me a gentle chuckle.

"Well, it's not that simple. Shannon's always been"—*like a mystical creature of fire and wings whose warmth is golden and feeds a part of you that has starved and you want more of her heat but she flies higher than you can ever reach for you are only a mortal being with legs of clay*—"out of my league."

John stared at me. His smile was gone and now his own brow was furrowed. He pointed to my laptop bag, made a motion with his fingers to suggest typing, then pointed at the books on the table and raised his eyebrows in a question.

"How did you know....? No, don't worry, forget it. You just know." I sighed. "It isn't anything serious. I just dabble here and there. I'm not attempting an award winning novel." I chuckled in self-deprecation.

He opened his hands in a querying gesture.

"Why not? Well, I....I mean, it's not like I can just sit down and come up with the next *Grapes of Wrath*."

John was silent but his gaze stayed upon me.

"What's your point, John?"

He wrote on his paper and tore me a scrap.

"Take care your hesitation does not invite the things you hesitate to avoid."

I closed my eyes and my mind filled. I saw a man in my office who was me, but older.

He was greying and his belly was soft and he cursed the lack of light and he groaned at the effort to climb down the stairs, and he walked to the Roastery and he sat at the table in the back and he worked on his emails and his eyes drifted to where Shannon walked and his eyes watered a little as she greeted visitors with a smile that was made every day for them and just for them.

I opened my eyes and I felt a prick of moisture at the edges of them. "Was that another stolen quote? I don't recognize it? Who was it?"

He said nothing. Only stared.

~

I walked into the Roastery the next morning. John's table was empty. Shannon walked over and said, "John didn't come today. Someone said they'd seen him walking out of town. It's a pity really, I liked him."

I said nothing and she said, "You want to go to your table and I'll bring you coffee?"

"You know what, Shannon? Why don't I sit right here for a change?"

She grinned. "Great idea. I never knew why you wanted to hide in the back there anyway."

I took out my laptop. As I opened the screen my emails showed. I clicked the 'close' button and opened Word. I took in a deep breath and began to type.

After a while, Shannon brought me my coffee and smiled as she put it down.

As she turned to leave my table I said, "Shannon, it's not too busy. Would Dorothy give you a few minutes to sit with me for a while? I'd love to talk with you."

The Box

Everything is faded or broken. The dull wallpaper that once paid homage to spring is a tired wash of faint markings that only hint of colours. The twisted floorboards are hazards that crack underfoot. The wooden cabinets have drawers that stick and doors that will not close.

The air is still, barely lit by lazy shafts of dusty light that the narrow windows reluctantly grant passage to.

A dark and narrow staircase opens into the space upstairs that was once *his* bedroom. Downstairs, at the back, is a cramped space that served as a second bedroom. *Where Elaine and I slept. How did we fit two cots?*

A passageway divides this room from the cramped kitchen and the sitting room, where a single yellow light provides a futile substitute for the lack of even a small window.

The largest room fills the entire front of the house, facing the short path from the road. It is his studio. Was his studio. Presumably once a grand porch, perhaps once a grand sitting room, it is graced with windows that wrap around front and sides. Compared to the rest of the dim house, the light here is good, if hazy with motes that float densely. But even here in this comparative chamber of light, the air is tinged by window glass that is greened with age.

His paintings are all around the studio. A few stand on easels for the occasional visitor to peruse. But most are on the floor, stacked against the walls.

As I look at them, I am reminded of when we were a family.

We lived in Annapolis Royal first. I don't remember our home there very well, but I know he had a proper studio and a real shop front displaying his art to passersby on the main road. I don't recall if he was a successful artist, but I suppose he sold enough to keep us well enough. Me, Elaine and our mother.

I don't remember our mother working then and I don't recall a life of luxury, but neither of hardship.

Back then I liked to spend time around him. Elaine and I would often have our own paints and papers scattered in the corner of his studio.

Annapolis is a popular draw for summer tourists. An elderly couple dropped in one day and slowly scrutinized the paintings while my father worked. The man coughed to get my father's attention and then remarked that he found the paintings quite angry.

I felt nervous when he said that, because it sounded insulting and I thought my father might be upset.

But he replied calmly. Dark, he said, doesn't mean angry. Dark is soulful, contemplative. Dark is dramatic. And dark makes occasional light all the brighter.

Those last words stuck in my young mind. Dark makes the occasional light all the brighter.

I recall the visitor seemed unimpressed by this answer and left. In truth, as I look around now, I see very little light radiating from those gloomy canvasses on which alizarins, umbers and ultramarines mix and muddy into gloomy tones.

I run my finger on one of the canvasses and it comes away coated with dust. I do the same on a few others.

They are all the same. These paintings have been undisturbed for a long time. I wonder how often he makes a sale these days, and how he has survived. Perhaps Joanne earned money in some way, until she left him, that is.

I think this out of curiosity, not concern. I haven't wondered at all if he has lived a life of comfort or hardship. The latter might be preferable. We had our share of hardships, after all, the three of us without him.

My phone rings.

"Hi. How's it going there?"

"Okay. It's weird, though."

"How so?"

"This place, it's pokey, depressing. And his paintings. I don't know what we'll do with them."

"Are they like they used to be?"

"Moody?" I tilt one or two of the paintings to see them more clearly. "Actually, worse. I can't imagine anyone wanting these on their walls."

"Well, there's something for everyone, hopefully. How are you holding up?"

"Not loving it. You should have come with me."

"I couldn't, you know that. Carl's away and—"

"You have to watch the kids. I know. But he was your father, too. We should be doing this together."

There's a silence at this. I think she might be sobbing and I don't know why.

"Elaine? You're not grieving, are you?"

She sniffs. "No, but I'm sad. I mean, we're supposed to feel something, and neither of us can. What does that say about us? It feels like there's a big gap in our lives where there should have been, you know, him."

"Yeah. Look, It is what it is. We made it here without him".

I pause but Elaine says nothing else.

I sigh, then. "Let me get finished here. I'll call you when I'm done."

Alone again, I leave the studio and make my way through the house. So far I've seen nothing that either Elaine or I would want to take ourselves. The only decisions for me seem to come down to what we could sell and what we have to haul away to the dump.

The paintings perplex me. I can't honestly see myself trying to sell them. I wouldn't know where to begin, or even if there would be a market for them. But I also feel a strange possessiveness over them. The idea of dumping them seems somehow very final.

I climb the stairs and survey his bedroom. There's a small double bed. Not even a queen. It's hard to see how two of them could have shared it comfortably, or did he downgrade to this after Joanne left him?

Not for the first time, I wonder why she left. Was he not the prize she thought he was when she stole him from us? Did she grow weary of this cramped and musty home? Did she finally see through the illusion and realize that he was, after all, just a mediocre artist with limited talent and little income?

There on the night-stand is a clutch of small framed pictures. Her, smiling confidently into the camera's lens. I'd heard people whisper that she was beautiful, as if that explained why he would abandon a wife and two small children, never to see them again. When I look at her smiling face, I can't see it.

Tucked behind it is one of the two of them together. They have been laughing and turned to each other. The camera catches them in that very intimate moment of shared happiness. I lay these frames face down.

There is one of me and Elaine. I would have been ten, eleven, maybe twelve. Elaine a little older but already smaller than me. I remember the picture. It was taken on Mavillette beach, on a perfect summer day. He was the one behind the camera. That had been a good day. He had been relaxed, playful even. Mother had not been there, I can't recall why.

I open the drawers and flick through the random assortment of useless items we all seem to accumulate in bedside drawers. I kneel to get to the bottom drawer and my eyes see the shoebox tucked away under the bed.

~

It is late evening now. A typical Nova Scotian sunset: the sun has dissolved into elaborate streams of violet and gold spreading across the horizon.

The light no longer filters into the house and I am dependent on the lamps that offer only thin pools of yellowish light. The house has no dining room, but a small, round breakfast table is squeezed into the corner of the kitchen, and there I sit.

The shoebox is on the floor beside me, empty. Its contents cover the table. Envelopes.

Most were addressed to him, in my mother's familiar handwriting.

I phone Elaine tell her what I have found.

"He kept letters she wrote to him? What kind of sadistic shit is that? What are they about?"

"Haven't opened any. Not sure I should."

"Jesus. You don't suppose she was begging him for help all those years."

"There's a few he wrote to her, too. Unopened, returned to sender."

"You sure they're his handwriting, not the witch's?"

"Joanne's?" We called her the witch for a long time when we were children. I think our mother said it first. I think there was a time we really believed she was one. "I couldn't say. I wouldn't know his writing, let alone hers."

"Well, you'd better open them."

"No."

"So what are you gonna do with them?"

"I dunno. Burn them?"

"So we'll never know?"

"Know what? We were there. You want to relive all that?"

For a while she is silent. This is something Elaine does when she disagrees with me but doesn't want to make it an issue. I know to let it go.

Eventually she sighs. "Look, you're the one there. It's your call. Whatever you decide."

"But you would read them?"

"Yes. But that's what I'm like, you know that."

I did. Elaine was terrier to my labrador. She couldn't let a thing pass without snapping and gnawing at it.

"I'm gonna burn them."

Sigh. "Okay. Talk later."

~

But twenty minutes later I'm still sitting at the table, staring at the jumble of envelopes.

We'll never know. Damn Elaine. Why does she have to be so unsettled? She's married now. With a kid. Why would she want to dig up the life we lived?

It was miserable. We barely scraped by financially. Mom worked as a housekeeper at some of the local hotels and inns around the area. In the winter months, very few accommodation businesses stayed open, so she claimed unemployment insurance. That wasn't much. The work in summer was minimum wage, and unlike waitressing it didn't come with good tips.

Our father never sent a cent, not even for the two of us.

We were *those* kids in school. The ones who never had the latest craze. Hell, we never had the old crazes already out of style. But being broke wasn't the hard part. We weren't the only family scraping by in the area.

What was hard for us was her bitterness. Something must have broken badly in her when he left her for Joanne, and it stole her empathy. She saw him when she looked at us, without a doubt. She was quick to snap at us, and often worse, for small things. She was physically strong, but emotionally damaged.

I begin to sort the envelopes by postage date until I have a chronological sequence. The first envelope seems to have been written soon after he left. I would have been around ten and Elaine twelve. The last, from her, is dated around the time Elaine and I were both out of high school and working in Halifax. So there's a few years spanned in front of me.

I'm intrigued, I'm afraid.

I reach for the first envelope and extract the letter inside. It is only a single page of handwriting scrawled on cheap lined paper, like they use in primary schools.

~

"Elaine."

"What is it?"

"You have to get here. Now."

"Brody, I've explained to you—"

"I don't give a shit about you and the what's going on with Carl."

"Jesus, don't talk to me like—"

"Elaine! I'm not kidding. You need to get in a car and drive out here. Right now."

That silence again, and then, in a softer voice, "you know it's at least a two-hour drive. I'll only get there around ten, at the earliest."

"Just get here," I whisper, and end the call.

It's almost eleven before I see headlights flood the front room and hear tires crunch to a halt on the road outside.

Elaine examines me closely as she passes me at the entrance. "Okay, I've got nothing but crap to deal with when I get back, but I'm here. What the hell is going on?"

I gesture towards the kitchen and follow her in. I've arranged the opened letters across the small table and the kitchen counter.

I move past her and take up the first paper, the one I selected earlier that day. "Read it."

She strains and frowns, glancing up at the light above.

"You'll get used to the light. The writing's not small."

I watch her face. It's only a few lines. But a long moment passes and she's still holding the paper, her face screwed in concentration. I see the paper begin to tremble in her fingers and a choking noise spurts from her. Her grip on the paper loosens and I take it from her as she is about to drop it.

"Sit," I tell her and hold the chair for her to do so.

"Brody, what the—?"

"I know. But that's only the start."

I place the first letter to one side and sit alongside her on another chair. She shakes her head, mumbles, "I, I don't get it."

I pick up the paper and read, slowly and deliberately.

So you've taken off like the chickenshit you are. What did you expect? You're a useless artist and a useless provider. You've been useless at everything, but you still think you could've fathered two healthy children like them? Run off and cry like a baby but it don't change nothing. You may not be their real father but you'll do right by me and them or I'll make your life a hell. Make sure I get a cheque from you soon.

Helen.

"Elaine. Tell me you understand what it says."

Her skin is blanched, her eyes abnormally wide, and glossy from tears that have begun to roll onto her cheeks. Briefly, she nods. "This is messed up, Brody." her voice is a coarse whisper.

"I know." Taking her hand, I ask her, "are you ready to see more?"

She nods.

"Elaine, it gets worse." I say softly.

Her eyes flash with panic now, but she nods.

I reach for the next letter in my organized trail.

> I heard what you did. Tried to see them, didn't you? You think I'm a fool? I told the school to watch out for you. You make sure you don't try that stunt again.
>
> And what's with that cheque? You think we'll manage with a couple of hundred? You're a useless excuse, but you'll find a way to do better than that. All I got to do is tell people you fiddled with the kids. And I'll tell the kids the same thing. I'll tell them over and over till they believe it. See how you handle that. Get me more money, now.

I'm watching Elaine's face as she reads, I feel moisture on my cheeks and brush it away, embarrassed.

"Oh god, Brody." She reaches over and squeezes my hand. "I'm so sorry you had to be on your own today."

I hand her the next letter. "This one is from him to her. She never opened it. 'Return to sender'."

She reaches for it and I pull it back. "Elaine, this one—"

She pulls it out of my hand. "Whatever this is, we handle it together, okay?"

Helen. I don't know what to do except beg. I'll find more money somehow. But please let me see Elaine and Brody. I can't just stop loving them even after what you told me. Please, Helen, think of what it will do to them if they think I've just abandoned them. I won't try to go behind your back. You can supervise my visits. Just don't cut me off, I beg you. For them.

Paul.

"Jesus. She didn't even read that? God, Brody. Our lives. Our whole fucking lives..." She doesn't finish the thought.

"There are a few more from him, spaced out over about three years. All similar. He tried Elaine, he really tried."

I'm not trying to choke back my tears now. I pick up a letter on the pile, screw it up and throw it across the room. Then I do the same with another. "She just keeps writing the same crappy demands and threats. Over and over. Elaine, how did we not know what kind of a shit she was?"

Elaine sits back in her chair, wiping her eyes and blowing her nose. She stares at the stack of letters she hasn't yet read, shrinks into herself.

"Deflection," she mumbles eventually. "It's the old politician's trick, isn't it? When you fail at something, tell your voters your opposition failed. When you break the rules, accuse the other guys of breaking the rules. Keep throwing your shit on them, just louder and more often than they do. The bigger the lie, the more chance people believe it, 'cause who would have the audacity to tell such a big lie? Who was it that said that? One of the Nazis, I think."

I nod. Then we looked at each other.

"Jesus," I let out with a sigh, "it was him used to talk to us about history, wasn't it?"

Her eyes well up again, she presses her lips together tightly as she nods.

"And those trips to the beach. It was only ever him, wasn't it?"

She nods again. "How did we wipe out those memories?"

"Do you want to read more?" I ask.

She shakes her head.

I put my hand on her shoulder and squeeze softly. "Probably best to get some sleep now."

Neither of us bother to shower or even change. We just lie down together on his bed. Elaine nestles against my shoulder. We sniff and sob until exhaustion overcomes us both.

I wake to a beam of sunlight pressing through the high window onto my face. I stumble downstairs to find Elaine at the table working through the letters.

"How long have you been up?" I ask as I fill the coffee machine with water.

Elaine gives me an impatient flap of the hand to quieten me. I busy myself with the coffee. I keep quiet until the coffee is brewed. I carry over two cups and sat one in front of her.

"I know why she left him."

"Joanne?"

Elaine nods. "He was a mess. You can feel it from his letters. He gets more and more desperate and even though he can see she's returning them unread he still keeps writing and pleading. He was obsessed with us, but he was terrified of what she would do. Jesus Christ, Brody, she threatened to accuse him of paedophilia with us! By the end, he was barely coherent. She totally dominated him, humiliated him. Brody, she broke him. I don't think Joanne could handle it anymore."

"Jesus. I feel sick." I did.

"Brody." she says as she fumbles for the coffee cup, her eyes locked on the paper in front of her. I quickly reach out and guide her hand to the handle.

She puts down the paper and looks at me. "All her letters demand money."

"Yes."

"Did you add them up?"

"How do you mean?"

"She keeps at him: this isn't enough, that isn't enough. Do more. Send more. This goes on for, what?" She reaches for the pile, her hands wafting over the papers till she finds one she is looking for. "Eight or nine years."

"Yeah, I know. She was hard on him."

"That's not the point. Brody. We lived a hard life. We weren't destitute, we weren't on the streets, but we weren't far off, were we?"

"Shit." Realization hits me.

"He sent money for all those years, pretty much until we were adults. He sent it for us, but—"

"What happened to it?"

We sit at the table, sipping coffee and staring into the dusted light. Images flash at me. Poorly darned socks that gave me blisters. Meals after meals after meals made of leftovers and leftovers and leftovers. Wearing Elaine's old shirts and the hysterical taunts of kids at school shouting "girly boy, girly boy." Elaine's clothes and mine packed easily in a small cupboard and her cupboard filled end to end with dresses and blouses and jackets and hats and shoes. Nights and nights spent on our own with only public-broadcast TV on a tiny screen, while she was out....

"Bingo." I say. "Those bingo nights. Remember them?"

"Jesus, yes. Were we stupid? How could we not have known?"

I don't have an answer, but Elaine nods anyway. "Meantime."

"Meantime."

After another pause, she says, "There's no way we'll ever know who he was, will we?"

"Our real father? I couldn't think where to begin."

Elaine reaches over and squeezes my leg. "There's something we can do, though"

"What's that?"

She reaches behind her and retrieves the picture I had turned over, the one with him and Joanne. She points at Joanne. "Find her, and say hello."

Changing Times

Mister Sprite sighed as the door closed behind the young girl. *Unsuitable. Again.*

The process of finding a new front desk attendant was proving more difficult than he had hoped. But he and Mister Ewan were of one mind. The first point of contact at the Harbourview Inn must be someone of superior character.

When the inn had first opened its doors in 1899, it had proudly advertised itself as a retreat for families of the better class. Two decades later, such a bold statement could no longer be made, not in this age of egalitarianism and enlightenment.

Mister Sprite shivered and gave his head a slight shake to clear his thoughts. *Perhaps the world is changing*, he thought. The great war had ushered in a new era, of aeroplanes, dirigibles and steamships that traversed oceans in days. Railways sprung up like weeds with untameable runners. Travel for leisure or business was no longer the reserve of the upper classes.

Mister Sprite had heard it said that common, working-class people were taking vacations just as their betters had done in the past. The thought of hosting such people disturbed him.

He walked to the door of his private quarters and gazed upon the grand inn looming over him. The site comforted him. *Our beloved inn still attracts its clientele from the distinguished and wealthy*, he thought.

The front desk attendant would be the first employee to engage with guests. The position required someone who reflected the superior manners and intellect of their guests.

Mister Ewan understood the difficulty Mister Sprite faced. Digby was a working-class town, and such qualities as polite language, intelligence and decorum were difficult to find. Mister Ewan trusted Mister Sprite to find the right person. Still, his patience would not be unlimited.

Mister Sprite's attention was suddenly captured by the sight of a girl scurrying at speed from the inn to the staff quarters.

"Ooh, there's the devil of a problem, Mister Sprite."

"Daisy, do not rush about so, and do not ever use such coarse language."

Daisy was hard-working and well-behaved. But she was a product of her time. Mister Sprite himself remembered when he was young. Crude language and lower manners had always been displayed freely amongst serving folk together. But they had always known to keep proper decorum around the finer classes and senior employees like himself. This new, enlightened generation either failed to recognize the walls that must exist between ranks, or they recognized but failed to acknowledge them.

Still, this was Harbourview Inn, and staff here would continue to know their place as long as he was the Manager.

"But Mister Sprite, it's the devil's work an' all. Come quickly, please!"

The lass was very earnest and scuttled off quickly. Mister Sprite set off after her. Fortunately his legs were considerably longer than the girl's and he was able to keep up with her with a reasonably dignified walk.

They made their way from the staff quarters to the kitchen entrance at the rear of the building. From there they entered the lobby. Mister Sprite coughed meaningfully. Daisy was wise enough to slow her pace and curtsy politely to the two guests who sat in the comfortable reading chairs. Mister Sprite followed with a polite smile and a smart nod of his head. Both guests were buried behind their newspapers and gave no acknowledgement of their presence or passing.

No matter, Mister Sprite mused, *it is important to maintain standards, whether seen or unseen.*

They passed through the lobby and entered the long annex where the dining room was located. It was a few minutes before noon. Mister Sprite was puzzled. Why was Daisy taking him to the dining room? At this time it would be empty. Apart from old Mister Fry of course.

Other guests, and some diners from the surrounding cottage community, would typically wander in around twelve thirty to one. Mister Fry liked to eat before all the others, having a distaste for noisy conversation while taking his victuals. Mister Sprite had always understood that and had urged the Inn's owners to be tolerant of Mister Fry's early arrival every day.

"What is it, Daisy?" Mister Sprite asked. Having left the lobby behind, Daisy had resumed her scuttle. This was quite unnecessary, as the dining room was located at the Inn's extremity and, as they were already in the dining room there could be no destination that required further scuttling.

Still, scuttle the girl did. Right across to the far end of the dining room, where gathered Vera and Ernest at Mister Fry's table.

At Mister Sprite's appearance they both stood smartly to attention, hands behind their backs. Mister Sprite acknowledged them with a slow tilt of his head. Vera performed a slight curtsy and Ernest a stiff bow from the abdomen, as was proper for his station.

"Mister Sprite," said Vera.

"Mister Sprite," said Ernest.

"Tshh," uttered Daisy.

Mister Sprite raised an eyebrow at this flagrant insubordination.

"Daisy!" he said in a carefully-controlled voice. "Your behaviour this morning is most unruly and unbecoming. Vera, you shall have words with Daisy."

Vera nodded.

Daisy said, "Tshh," again.

Despite Mister Sprite straining an eyebrow in the most intimidating fashion, Daisy pointed past Vera and Ernest to where Mister Fry sat.

"He ain't moving, Mister Sprite," Daisy said impatiently, and a little loud.

"Hush, Daisy. Ain't right to raise your voice so," Vera interrupted.

Mister Sprite graced Vera with a slight nod and once again turned to Daisy with an imposing eyebrow.

Daisy's eyes opened wide. She took in a breath and actually stamped a foot.

"Daisy!" Mister Sprite protested.

"Daisy!" echoed Vera

"Oh Daisy," said Ernest in a worried tone.

Daisy was surprisingly unperturbed by their collective disapproval.

Mister Sprite said to Vera, "A serious discussion with Daisy is required. Her lack of decorum and respect this morning is unbecoming to an establishment of the standing of Harbourview Inn. Daisy, you will listen carefully to Vera and moderate your behaviour accordingly. Or there shall be consequences."

"Mister Sprite!" Daisy called out with urgency and surprising confidence for someone who was being discussed by the Matron and Manager, no less.

As Mister Sprite turned to face her, he attempted the most severe and intimidating eyebrow lift he could imagine. But he found himself caught between different options and instead faced her with eyes twitching like a fool.

"Mister Sprite!" Daisy said again, her tone sharp, critical even. His breath caught in his throat. Daisy's defiance was staggering.

Mister Sprite found himself lacking a response to it. He gasped, audibly and let his jaw drop open like a simple-minded commoner. He was mortified by his display of common behaviour. He resolved to confess his shortcomings to Mister and Mrs. Ewan.

"Mister Sprite." Daisy's tone was now pleading. Mister Sprite felt a modicum of his authority return.

"What is it, Daisy?" He asked after clearing his throat with a deliberately gruff and, he hoped, disapproving note.

"He's dead, Mister Sprite."

"I don't follow," said the Inn's Manager with the air of someone who had just been told the moon had merged with the sun. This young creature was well liked by guests who found her exuberance charming. But she came from a simple background in which people no doubt viewed life in simple ways. *Dead*, he thought. *I wonder what that word means in the lexicon of the poor and disadvantaged.*

"Dead, Mister Sprite. Expired. Deceased. No longer of the living world. At one with—"

"Yes, yes, yes," he interrupted. "But he cannot simply be, well, dead."

Daisy looked first at Vera, then at Ernest. Neither raised their head from the supplicant stances they had taken as soon as Daisy had interrupted their senior. Mister Sprite concluded that either Daisy had lost her mind, or was onto something and the other two were too timid to say anything.

In spite of both of them outranking Daisy, he found himself leaning towards the latter conclusion. At the very least, Daisy's incredible claim merited his personal investigation. He was, after all, Manager of this fine establishment.

"Move aside, all of you." Mister Sprite's voice was at its commanding best and they all obeyed.

He took a stride forward. There was Mister Fry, sat in his usual chair at his usual table, right in the far corner facing the remainder of the dining room, so there was no possibility of anyone sitting behind him. This was all perfectly normal. Perhaps Daisy had lost her mind?

However, Mister Fry was remarkably quiet, considering the four of them were standing around him, interrupting his luncheon with a conversation about his demise.

Mister Sprite took one more tentative step and leaned forward slightly. "Mister Fry. I trust you are enjoying your luncheon as usual?" This seemed the appropriate way to communicate with a valued customer who may or may not have passed beyond his cognitive state.

There was no reply. Mister Sprite leaned forward a little more and peered at his eyes. A pointless effort, as it turned out. The gentleman's eyes were quite closed.

"Ahem, Mister Fry. Do not be alarmed, but I shall gently shake your arm to waken you." This seemed sensible, as it was more than probable the gentleman had inadvertently dozed off.

Mister Sprite then reached out his hand and pushed Mister Fry's arm back and forth a tiny measure. He thought he heard a faint exclamation of impatience from Daisy, but when he glanced at her sharply she had her mouth squeezed tightly shut.

Mister Sprite turned his attention back to the gentleman in front of him. He cleared his throat. "Ah, Mister Fry. Mister Fry, do wake up, sir."

Mister Fry did not stir.

"Er, Mister Sprite." Vera had learned to soften the edges of her spiky Scottish brogue and, when needed, could modulate it into a reassuring tone of authority and common sense. "I know the lass is perhaps being a tad disrespectful, but I believe she has the right of it. Our Mister Fry here has indeed passed away. I dinna think he will respond to neither inquiries nor urgings."

Mister Sprite straightened himself. He glanced at Ernest, who bowed his head, whether to agree with Vera or simply to avoid Mister Sprite's scrutiny, he could not be sure. Then he glanced at Daisy, who had the sensibility to stare at the floor.

Last, Mister Sprite turned to Vera and nodded. "Well," he proclaimed, "this is an unprecedented situation."

"What should we do, Mister Sprite?" asked Vera.

"Do?"

"Do."

Mister Sprite realized his subordinates expected him to have a course of action ready for such a situation. He suddenly felt a tightening in his chest. It was most inconvenient of Mister Fry to pass away in such unusual circumstances.

"Well," he stroked his chin in an attempt to appear thoughtful. He needed a moment to think. For some reason, his mind felt quite sluggish, and he held his thoughtful pose for an uncomfortable period.

"We should tell the hospital. They'll need to send a van, I'd say." It was Daisy.

Damn, can the girl not know her place? Mister Sprite turned to her with his most exasperated expression. His eyebrows were positively contorted now. "Miss Fay!" Using her formal name in a sharp tone was surely a sign to her that she was overstepping her station. "You go too far! Mind your place and speak when spoken to."

Now something happened that Mister Sprite could not have envisaged in any circumstances. Daisy spoke back to him as sharply as he had spoken to her.

"Mister Sprite! You are on and on about my manners like it's the only thing important happening here and now. But there"—she pointed a finger at Mister Fry—"sits a corpse, a dead man. And,"—she now raised her finger at Mister Sprite, the temerity of it causing him to feel a rush of blood to his face. He opened his mouth to admonish her again but she continued stridently—"And in only ten minutes this room will fill with folks seeking their lunch and being alarmed at the site of a dead body in their eating place."

Daisy crossed her arms defiantly. Ernest resembled a corpse himself, his blood having drained from his face. Vera's eyes were wide, but she shifted over to Daisy and put an arm around the girl's waist.

"Mister Sprite," Vera began. But Mister Sprite interrupted her.

"Yes, yes. I see the difficulty. We shall have to inform Mister and Missus Ewan".

"They will have to be woken," Vera spoke. "It's a mite early for them yet."

Vera was right. Lunch was a casual affair at which guests and cottage owners could mingle informally. The Ewans would make their grand entrance for a late-afternoon aperitif with guests, and then join them for a formal dinner followed by cocktails at the bar. The Ewans and their guests would dress in formal black tie each evening. This mingling of important guests with the owners of such a fine establishment was a tradition deeply etched into the reputation of the Inn.

Waking the Ewans at lunchtime was simply not done.

Mister Sprite cleared his throat again. "Ernest, you shall go to the third floor and knock on Mister and Mrs. Ewan's door. Inform them of the situation."

More blood visibly drained from Ernest's face and his hands began to tremble. He seemed weak at the knee as well, as he stumbled in place.

"No." Of course, it was Daisy, strangely commanding. "Ernest must take the car to the hospital."

Of course, Mister Sprite cursed inwardly. He should have thought of that. Besides Mister Ewan himself, Ernest was the only one capable of driving the infernal thing.

Ernest regained some colour and eagerly nodded to indicate his willingness.

"Yes, yes. Go!" Mister Sprite instructed him. "But stay away from acquaintances, and mind you inform the hospital of Mister Fry's demise in terms that cast no shadow on our institution."

Ernest stood with mouth gaping. His colour was draining again.

"Oh, for heaven's sake, just go straight to the hospital and tell them an elderly guest appears to have passed away and request an ambulance. Dinna say a word more or less than that and ye'll be grand." Vera's no-nonsense common sense was finding its voice at the right time.

Ernest nodded vigorously and set off.

"Well," Mister Sprite began, "ah, now we, ah," but his brain had relapsed into that vaguely ineffective state again.

Daisy moved around to the back of Mister Fry's chair. She signalled Vera, who came to one side of the chair. "Mister Sprite, would you mind?" Daisy asked.

Mister Sprite could not help feeling that her tone was slightly tolerant, a touch condescending. But he looked over and Daisy was gesturing for him to take the side opposite Vera's. He did so.

Then Daisy called, "all right, let's lift."

She and Vera both lifted the chair on which Mister Fry sat. Hurriedly, Mister Sprite followed suit and lifted his side. Mister Fry sat on his chair, precariously balanced between the three of them. Daisy tilted the chair backwards so she bore more of the weight, and the corpse rested against the backrest.

"Right, out the back door," Daisy said.

The back door? Mister Sprite was alarmed. Guests and cottage owners did not enter or exit from the back door. He opened his mouth to protest, but Daisy and Vera were already moving that way and he found himself forced to follow.

Crab-like, they manoeuvred the body and chair to the back door and, with some difficulty, out the door and down the short flight of steps to the path below.

"Now, to the arbour," Daisy said.

"To the arbour?" Mister Sprite exclaimed and placed his side of the chair on the path. Vera had no choice but to follow him. "We cannot place Mister Fry in full view of everyone who walks past the front of the Inn!" he exclaimed, feeling his authority was returning.

Daisy sighed. She set down the back of the chair and pulled a book out of her apron pocket. She held it up triumphantly. It was *The Grapes of Wrath. An excellent, if disturbing read,* Mister Sprite thought. *But surely not to Daisy's taste?* He looked puzzled.

"It's his book!" Daisy proclaimed. "What he reads every day, after lunch. Under—"

"Under the arbour," Vera said with a smile.

"Under the arbour," Mister Sprite concurred.

Two minutes later, Mister Fry was to be seen sitting in his favourite spot under the delightful shade of the arbour, apparently absorbed in his latest novel. Not many greeted him, as they knew his preference for peace and quiet on a nice afternoon. Those who did and received no response noted that his eyes were closed and concluded he had succumbed to the soporific climate.

When Ernest returned, he reported that the ambulance was only a few minutes behind him.

Mister Sprite was appalled. He had no idea how ambulances worked, but he had assumed they would be very busy, and would arrive long after the diners had departed and guests had taken to their rooms for their afternoon naps. As it was, the dining room was now half full, and many of the diners would have a view of the arbour and the activities that were about to scandalize it.

He was about to admonish Ernest to turn around and find some way to delay the ambulance. After all, the body in question was already deceased. No amount of hurry could make Mister Fry's situation any better.

But as he was about to talk to Ernest, Daisy skipped towards the dining room.

Mister Sprite turned to Vera in bewilderment. "What is the girl doing now?" he asked desperately.

Vera only shrugged.

Then they saw Daisy appear in the dining room. She said something to the diners that caught their attention and made them laugh. Mister Sprite and Vera moved closer to the window so they could see and hear. Daisy made a joke of admonishing a guest whose plate was only half finished. "No pudding for you, dear." She wagged her finger.

The other diners chuckled.

Then Daisy moved to another table. "Ooh," she exclaimed, "look at this gentleman's plate. Not a drop left. He shall have a hug from me."

Although her words were scandalous, they were directed at a man probably in his eightieth year, or more. He grinned broadly at the flirtatious attention, and the dining hall clapped their approval at the show.

Daisy continued her tour of the dining room, with lots of laughter following her movements.

The ambulance arrived. Fortunately, it did not sound one of those horrible sirens. But still it was a garish-looking vehicle.

Mister Sprite directed it to park as much as possible behind the cover of the arbour's bushes. But he need not have worried. Daisy had the diners enthralled with her display of flirtatious humour. No one was looking out of the window.

The transfer of the body was a quick affair and, within a few minutes, the ambulance was gone.

~

"Splendid work, Sprite!" Mister Ewan held his hands behind his stiffened back in his customary military posture. In fact, he had no military background at all, but cultivated the appearance of one. He avoided any conversation related his service, changing the subject whenever a guest raised it. This projected an enigmatic image of someone whose service had been of a secret nature. That image appealed to the privileged type who spent their holidays at Harbourview Inn.

"Now, we just need a plan for what to tell Fry's family. No doubt they'll notice his absence in a short while."

"Ah, Mister Fry vacations alone each year, Mister Ewan. He has no family in attendance at his cottage." This was probably something Sprite's employer should have known, but it was not Sprite's place to judge his superiors.

"Ah, yes, well, capital then. You shall draft a suitable letter for me to sign and post to his family. Sad event but peaceful passing and all that."

Mister Sprite nodded and offered a small bow, as was his habit when taking instruction from his employer.

"Well then, unfortunate business but managed as well as can be. Carry on, Sprite." Mister Ewan turned his back to Mister Sprite and made to stride off.

"Ahem," Mister Sprite coughed, just enough to cause Mister Ewan to turn.

"What is it now, Sprite?" The tone was irritable.

"It's about the Front Desk Attendant position, sir."

"What? Don't tell me you've finally found someone in this commoners' playground?"

"Actually, sir, we seem to have had the right person here all along."

Mister Ewan frowned and lifted an eyebrow to invite Mister Sprite to explain.

"I shall be appointing Daisy to the position, sir."

The Summit

There, at last. The summit. A thousand years. No, a thousand and a thousand years. More. The decades and centuries and millennia by which people marked their passages had long since lost meaning.

In the beginning, there was only a journey to be made, with a destination so far away it was beyond imagination, even for him. But the idea of it inside his head drove him all through these ages, it haunted him and it sustained him.

And here it was at last, in his sight. An opening. No gate of gold, no pillars of marble, no guardian at the ready. Just an opening from which flowed the mountain he had climbed these past ages.

If he had known what the journey would be like, would he have taken that first step? He asked himself that question every day, every hour. The journey of unending climb and toil had punished his body and tested his will.

In the beginning, his determination gave him energy and purpose. His legs powered through the thick, cloying sourness, and the climbs over hardened residues were quickly mounted and left behind.

But then followed so much tiredness. Tiredness was his enemy and his beloved companion.

The stuff flowed and set, sometimes it began to set as he strode on it, and it clung to his feet and came up in long strands as he pulled away. One climb was mounted. Another lay ahead. And another, and another, and every muscle, every nerve, every thought begged for rest. For a thousand and a thousand and a thousand years, and more and more. Until the tiredness and pain became existence itself.

When he began to thrive on his pain, his steps grew stronger and faster. Each step forced through that torrent of death would be a step never made again. Resolve became determination again, and in his determined state he breathed the corrupted air and took energy from it. He discovered ways to twist and turn his body to make better progress through the cloying rushes. He progressed.

Through all this, at all times, he observed the chaos below and around. Because there lay the purpose.

Now, at last, he paused. Here the seemingly endless mountain narrowed towards its summit, and its source was revealed. An opening, from which poured the sickly air so thick it became liquid. Here the strength of the torrent was at its worst.

He paused and watched as the river of it billowed from the opening to pour down the mountain, where it would become the mountain itself. Endless and constantly growing.

He felt his pain and the tiredness disappear at the sight of the end, and he felt oddly weakened by the loss of them. His legs gave under him, and he sank to his haunches.

Immediately the stuff began to reach for him, and he angrily slapped it away.

Just beyond the opening was his destination. And there lay his real struggle, for which he could never be prepared. He felt he should rest before he faced the opening and what lay beyond.

But he was afraid to rest. Never mind the desperate stuff that feared its own decaying end and clung to life in any form. Rest is determination suspended, an invitation to doubt. Doubt becomes despondency and return to banishment, which would be the end of all things.

He pushed through a clinging wave, and another. And the opening was finally in his reach.

At its source, the opening was small, just large enough to squeeze through with body bent. He stood in front of it. The flow assailed him with a roar. The roar was not loud in his ears, but he felt its fire burn his skin, and its edge knifed deep into his flesh.

He lifted his hand to test the flow, and it was stronger by far than the waves he had yet braved. He crouched and made an attempt to push his way through, but the force of it beat him back.

He squatted and focused his mind. He took in deep breaths, taking care to turn his head upwards and away from the oceans below, which might be enraged by his struggles. He coaxed his body to settle. Then, becalmed and ready, he pushed into the opening's flow.

The sour stench was greater now, the force pounded at him, and the clamminess dragged at him cruelly. But he had suffered a thousand thousand waves, and he had learned to draw his inner strength and to use his body against the flow.

It was harder now, but his strength drove him, so his feet pushed forward an inch and then an inch and then an inch. And suddenly he was through the torrent and his journey of an eternity was done.

It was a plain room. No, not a room. A cave, used as a room. Inside the room there was no evidence of the flow that had forged a mountain below. Dust thickly covered the stone floor.

As he stepped into the room, a cloud of dust spat up and whirled, offended to be disturbed. He stepped again, placing his feet with care but still raising clouds around his feet.

He gazed around him. The walls were shaved from solid rock, as was the ceiling. No ornamentation, no carvings, no lighting. Just an opening scraped from a solid mass. It was as he remembered, then. But for the books.

They were new. Huge mounds of books, stacked around the

floor, towers of them leaning against the walls of stone. Some of the stacks were covered in blankets of dust that flowed from the top book to the bottom. Some stacks seemed newer, one or two were topped by books that appeared newly printed and bound.

It sat in the centre of this cave of books, sprawled in a chair fashioned from the same stone as the cave itself. Its throne. Its robes, being eternal, were still fine and vivid, but the way the folds hung so loosely betrayed the wasted body within.

It turned its head, apparently with great effort. "You," it said with a voice become dust itself. It frowned, a visible effort at recollection. "I cast you down."

He nodded. "And here I am."

"Hmph," it snorted, "I shall cast you again."

It waved a derisive hand, but the movement was feeble.

He walked forward, pausing before the throne to gaze at it, taking in the changes. He was shocked. All these years he had imagined the immense task ahead of him. He had not expected this....husk.

He moved to one of the walls and examined the piles of books. Here and there he rubbed away the dust.

"So much dust," he said, his tone a question.

"What of it?" it asked. "Dust is the remains of life."

"And these?" He lifted one of the books. It was bound in ancient leather. It was cracked and brittle, but when he opened it to the pages within, the beauty of its calligraphy and illustration caught his breath.

He heard a small gasp from the throne. He glanced back and saw panic in its eyes, that he might damage the book. He closed it and placed it back.

"These are their testimonies of devotion?" he asked.

It only shrugged, feigning indifference, but its eyes still shifted to the book he had held.

"Why have you returned?" it asked.

"Once there were angels here," he said. "This place was filled with their light."

"Ah," it sighed. "My most divine."

"Divine. Being in praise of god, or like a god."

"Not *like* a god!" it snapped. "One God, many devotees."

He snorted. "Devotees, yes. And where are they now, those devotees, those fanatics?" He shivered for a moment. "Those brutish slaves thirsting for...what?" He waved his arm as he searched for the right word. "Your acknowledgement?"

"They loved me!" it spat, sounding like sun-dried leaves crushed in the hand.

"They worshipped you," he replied.

"The same," it said dismissively.

"No. Not the same. And that"—he stood before it—"that is everything, is it not? That is why I returned."

It looked up at him. Its face was nothing like the radiant and beautiful vision he remembered. This was a face disfigured by lines, filthy with unwashed dust and with flesh that hung loose. But the eyes still held power.

Be careful, he warned himself.

The eyes glared at him with warning and hate, but he saw in there a hint of fear as well.

He crouched so that his eyes were on a level with its eyes. "Did you know that I began my journey back the very moment I landed where you had me cast? I saw the climb I faced and knew it was impossible, and yet, I began it. Immediately. Did you know that, all-knowing? Did you see it, all-seeing?"

"You think I am finished," it croaked. "You bided your time 'til you thought me weak. But you are wrong. See! I am regaining strength as we speak!"

It lifted its left hand and showed its fingers. Its hand was near skeletal and the skin translucent. And it shook uncontrollably. But it strained, and the index finger it pointed forward was solid, strong, youthful.

"Ah," he said, nodding in acknowledgement of the finger. He leaned forward, his mouth against its ear. "What allure has light? Do you remember?" he whispered.

It pulled away from him and hissed.

"You still feed on them," he said to it.

"There is love for me yet!" it protested.

"Worship," he stated flatly.

"The same," it said petulantly.

He sighed and turned away from it. He turned his gaze to the walls and floor, looking not at them, but beyond them.

The rock and dust faded to nothing, as if they were illusions. Now, instead of a cave, he floated in a space that hovered inside but also outside a teeming mass of humanity. He contemplated them for a time, fascinated by the rush and chaos as they so quickly spent their little lives.

"There are so many now, so many more than before, and so widely spread," he commented.

It tilted its head in acknowledgement.

"And yet you fade," he added.

It fixed him with eyes blazing. For a moment he felt an old stab of fear. *I am so much stronger than it now*, he thought. But he remembered the power it once wielded and took a cautionary step backwards.

"I have watched, you know. On my journey here. I lacked your grand view from my path, but I saw some of it," he said. "They have a mad, senseless history, don't they?"

"You have seen their love for me, then," it stated as a matter of fact.

"Worship!" he shouted, and when it flinched instead of rising up to him, he felt stronger. Despite all he had spent of himself to reach this place, he felt himself renew.

He crouched in front of it again. "They ran into battles with your name screaming from their lungs. They cared nothing if their bodies were trampled in rivers of flesh and blood, because their souls would be yours. They threw themselves on fires and burned with ecstasy in their eyes because your name was on their lips as the flames boiled their flesh. They sacrificed their own children and thought it a good deed, for you had commanded it. Oh, what they would sacrifice for the chance to die and be an angel at your side."

Its eyes closed and it took in a deep breath. He knew it was basking in the memories of those times.

"Those creatures"—he pointed towards the billions of lives surrounding them—"they have in them a singular lust for blood. But it suited you well, did it not? A terrible death in your name is so much more appetizing than a quiet passing away in the night."

It kept its eyes closed. Perhaps it was still basking in memories, perhaps childishly closing out his voice as it had done so often in the past.

"But they have changed. What do they offer you now, hmm?" he taunted. "They no longer die for you. They get rich for you!"

He laughed and took pleasure in the grimace that flickered on its face. "And they hate for you. In so many ways. For you, they hate styles of dress, designs of temples, choices of words, their own science, and who to support in their trivial leadership squabbles."

He leaned forward so that his face was close to its, so that it would feel his breath upon its withered skin. "No wonder you have shrunk to this."

He waved his arm with contempt at it, sunk into its pathetic throne of rock and dust. "They are so many now, yet not one of them would offer you their death," he snarled. "They would not even offer you their meaningless fortunes."

He looked around the empty room and said, "Of all those billions, not a single one is willing to become your angel, your assassin."

It opened its eyes now. The eyes were still the most potent part of it, and even now capable of demanding his attention. Its eyes fixed on his and he felt its petulant defiance.

"You think I am done," it croaked, "but there is still love for me and I can reach its power. Be on guard, for I am always and forever." It hissed these words, full of venomous warning.

He stood again. *Be careful with it*, he thought again.

Before he was cast down, he had spent many lifetimes in its thrall. He had seen it murder its own father to become ruler of its fellow deities. He had watched its worship addiction grow alarmingly, until it was insatiable. He had seen it grow jealous of the devotions offered to other Olympians.

Then he had witnessed the terrible carnage of the other gods, after its interest had fixated on a small desert tribe that believed in the strange idea of a single god.

It was a subtle movement that he almost missed. Its hand lifted just a little, moving over the panorama of humanity in which they floated. It wavered with indecision, before lazily selecting a small land mass jutting off the east coast of a continent.

"No!" he shouted, but it was too late. The finger had twitched faintly while pointing to a small town near where a great mass of water squeezed through a narrow land gap.

He followed the finger's direction and made himself descend.

In an instant he stood in the midst of destruction. A brutal wind hammered into him from multiple directions, its awful howl competing with a dreadful mix of other sounds. Rain armoured with shafts of ice thudded and hammered against any solid surface. Metal shrieked as it was torn apart by vicious winds. Vehicles lifted and crashed as they were flung in all directions. Hidden behind whatever shelters they could find, people screamed. From somewhere came the sound of waves smashing with devastating force.

He stilled the air immediately around him to create a bubble of calm. He tried to extend his bubble, but could only push it a short distance. Inside it, he turned to take in the chaos around him.

He was in the middle of a road, with the remains of shops on both sides. Vehicles were strewn haphazardly, piled upon each other, with some smashed into buildings. Everywhere, glass was shattered by the icy rain, the winds and the wreckage.

To his left he saw a body of water rise far above the rooftops of the buildings and smash into them, breaking them apart and scattering them as if they were paper. There were many more waves angrily pulsing towards the town.

A metal statue flew past him. The human obsession with making likenesses of their gods had done much to feed the addictions of the gods themselves. The sustenance provided by just one statue or painting could nourish a god for many human years. Then they began to make likenesses of their own human leaders and heroes, and the gods had starved and weakened.

He slowed the flight of this statue and read the inscription on its base. The statue was of a soldier and meant to represent the many men of this town, Digby, who had died in some meaningless war that was only one of so many wars these humans waged against each other.

Pointless, he thought.

He watched it fly until it landed on the hard road surface and broke apart, smashed to splinters by the elements.

Then suddenly it was over. The wind faded in an instant, the waves subsided and the sea calmed. The riot of sounds became a silent fog, through which only screams penetrated. It was as if the storm's source of energy had suddenly failed.

And indeed, he knew it had.

He followed the screams, finding a group of humans in a large concrete building. He moved towards them.

There were raised voices as well now, shouting down the screamers. "Quiet! It's over! Listen!"

There was a quiet moment when the screamers paused, faces peered out of windows, where windows had survived. Then the screamers became wailers. They cried, out of fear, out of loss, out of relief.

He felt their agony and it gave him pain.

He entered the building and moved among them, though they did not know it. He saw a man bawling like an infant. In his arms lay the limp body of a child. The man's pain weakened him.

He knelt and placed his hand upon the man's shoulder, though the man would not know it. He placed his other hand upon the child's corpse.

He searched for its final pain and drew it into himself, then watched as the child left its body, pausing for a moment to glance at him before floating away to join the mountain flow.

He wanted to spend more time in this town it had destroyed, doing the job he had missed for so many ages. But he knew his task was greater than this and he pushed himself back to the barren cave.

It was even more fragile now. Its arms hung limply by its side, its head lolled sideways.

"You fool!" he spat. "You arrogant, narcissistic fool! Did you waste those lives, and what little power you had left in you, just to prove a point to me?"

It lifted its head a fraction and produced a smile which, although strained, was also triumphant. Its finger pointed feebly to the scene in Digby. People were emerging from their hiding places, they gazed with bewilderment at the inexplicable destruction all around them.

Someone called out a plaintive, "Why?"

More cried out, "Oh god, why?"

Then a voice shouted, "thank God for saving us!"

Other voices chimed in, "Amen, amen!"

People knelt, pressing their hands together and lifting their eyes to the sky.

A woman dropped to her knees while the man with her shook his head and continued to stand. But she grasped him by his pants and spoke to him, and he finally knelt with her.

He shook his head at the convoluted logic of these human. Despite all the progress they had made, all their science and discovery, they remained superstitious creatures, afraid of the dark and needing to believe something watched over them when the light is gone.

He turned to look at it. A breeze that did not move the air floated around him, rising from the growing numbers of people praying on the ravaged streets below. The breeze passed into it and its appearance changed.

Colour returned into its face. The dust-choked lines that patterned its face filled out and smoothed. Its body straightened and flexed with muscles newly redeveloped.

The people below began to gather their dead. He felt the pull of their restless souls. Those living prayed some more over the bodies of their loved ones, begging for forgiveness of their sins from the one who had just slaughtered them.

One woman began to shriek and beat herself on her chest. Someone tried to restrain her but she pushed them off. "Lord, forgive me," she screamed, "forgive me my sins. Let me dedicate my life to your service. I will worship you and take no earthly thing above you."

She tore at her clothing, desperately throwing them aside, as if her nakedness was a gift to her god.

A strong, glowing thread wafted up from the woman to join the breeze. It joined with many other threads that wove together. They entered it and it shuddered, then rose to its feet. At its full height it was much of what it once had been. It was impressive and intimidating.

He stood his ground, as he knew he must, but caution surged through him.

When it spoke, its voice was as if it travelled from the deepest caves buried under great mountains. He felt it pulse on his skin as much as he heard it.

"I cast you down," it repeated, questioning and accusing.

"Yes. And I climbed back."

"I should have ended you."

"As you did the others."

It shrugged. Inconsequential, the shrug said.

"Your memory is as broken as the rest of you," he told it. "You had no need to eliminate me. I never needed the living and their adoration the way you did, and those you slaughtered. All this"—he waved his hand at the books, and the desperate voices of worship still faintly rising—"was nothing to me. I was no competition to you, unlike my dear brothers and sisters." He glared at it, but it was unmoved.

"But there was a more important reason to let me live," he said. He waited for some recognition, but there was none. *Are its shoulders beginning to sag again?*

"You needed my existence," he continued, and that impassive face broke into a small frown. "What allure has light?" he waited, but although it narrowed its eyes, there was still only puzzlement.

"Do you not remember your words?" he shouted. "What allure has light if not against darkness?"

There was a tilt of its head, a moment of recognition, at last. Then it took in a breath and sighed."Yes," it rumbled. "You are my darkness."

"As you assigned us, yes."

"But you troubled me."

"I challenged you. I begged you to end your slaughter. I begged you to end your torture of those limited creatures."

"You think it a torture for them to love me?" it roared. It seemed to raise itself up higher, those sagging shoulders suddenly flexed, and despite himself he was intimidated.

But it was a momentary change. The cries of adulation from below were already fading, and the bright tendrils floating around it were thinning. The awesome posture began to soften.

He shook his head. "There is no need for us to debate this again. You have had your time, and it is done."

Its eyes widened. It raised and pointed its finger at him, and bellowed as loud as it could, "I cast you down again!"

A glimmer of pearlescent light floated from the pointed finger, but it was a soft light that moved languidly. He watched it float gently towards him, then blew on it as it neared and the light shimmered and splintered into nothing.

Its body began to shrivel and it collapsed into the stone throne again. Now it was even more frail than it had been when he had entered just a short time ago. The use of its power on that poor town had taken far more than it had gained.

"Look at you," he spat. "What have you not used to squeeze more worship? Once you inspired, but your nature kept exposing you. Was there ever a time you could resist a human virgin? You intimidated, but they found heroes. You tried love and sacrifice for a time, but you had little stomach for it. The afterlife fantasy always worked well for you. But terror has always been your preference, not so?"

It sagged, spent, and did not respond.

"But they have changed. They are not the primitive mass they once were. Too many among them have learned to see, to think, to understand. Even your terror moves only some of them, and it is not enough to sustain you. And they have found greed. Greed is a far more powerful god to them than you."

He glared at it. His anger boiled inside of him. He wanted to tear it apart with his hands. This tyrant was broken and wasted.

But he held himself back. *This must be done right, so that the end can be the beginning.*

"Enough," he said.

He walked to the first pile of books, and slowly past them, dragging his fingers across the tops of the piles, and he spoke softly to them as he passed. "Give up your truths, enlightenment and love. All else be ashes."

A line of flames followed his fingers, rapidly engulfing the impressive walls of books.

It groaned loudly behind him, an animalistic noise, bathed in pain. But he paid it no mind, instead observing the flames. Here and there, some pages and fragments of pages were spat out from the flames, to land untroubled in the thick dust that coated the floor, but the vast bulk turned to ashes in moments.

He thrust his hand into the fire, taking hold of a viscous, almost liquid thread of flame. He dragged it and aimed it at the walls in front of the throne. "See!" he shouted.

It wailed a desperate cry, "Nooooo!"

The liquid flame burst against the cave walls and consumed them. In a matter of moments, the walls of the cave disappeared. Once again, the world of humanity was revealed. But this time, it was as if a one-way mirror had been burned away. The scene in the cave was revealed to those below, just as they were revealed themselves.

"What have you done?" Its voice was cracked and filled with terror.

Across the globe, billions of people suddenly paused their activities and gaped at the sight. An image surrounded them, somehow above them and below them and all around them. It was disorienting and the mass of humanity fell to its knees in a wave of nausea and disbelief.

As their brains adjusted, they saw an impossibly old and frail creature. For a moment, each one of them thought the creature was just like them. But a moment later they thought it looked like others. Then, they had a sense that it was actually like none of them at all, but tried to be all of them at once and was terribly deformed for it.

The creature slumped upon a large seat that seemed carved from stone. It struggled to pull itself upright. It moved its lips, and its voice floated over them in a myriad of languages. "Behold, I am your...."

But the deep, rich strength of the first syllable collapsed into a dry whisper, and its sentence hung, unfinished as its head fell forward.

Another figure stepped forward out of the shadows. This one was stronger. He appeared dark, serious. At first he seemed menacing. He held in his hands a pile of scrap. No, not scrap. Pages and fragments of paper. Some printed, some with words drawn by hand.

Someone cried out to the dark one, "My Lord, I am your servant. Bless me." More voices cried out raise similar chants.

The dark one held up a hand to silence them. "No!" he shouted. "No more."

He cast the pages into the atmosphere. They floated and then burst into a billion fragments of light that moved gracefully like tiny stars.

The dots of light passed through the people and then were gone, but everyone felt an instant of insight they would spend their lives trying to understand.

As their minds accepted these insights, the old and frail one slowly disintegrated, as if it were a statue of sand that had dried out and collapsed in on itself. Particles of it fell with gathering speed, until there was no form of it left.

Then the dark one gazed upon them all, tilted forward and fell. He fell from above them, from below them, from around them. But he fell a great distance and landed with a great thud that threw up dust right amongst them, wherever they stood.

Across the globe, they gathered around a corpse that was just a corpse. They looked up and around and the opening to the heavenly cave was gone.

For a time, the world was silent. Most were frozen in shock, unable to process what they had witnessed. Most felt afraid. Most felt a sense of being alone. But they were puzzled and intrigued by new thoughts in their heads.

They began to find each other, and to talk.

Acknowledgements

To my son, Jordan, who gifted me a writing course and thus gave me a gentle push down this path.

To Andrew and the Moose House team, for teaching me that editing is an art form that can make a story better without really changing it.

About the author

Greg Metcalf grew up in northern England, an avid reader and lover of history. Moving to South Africa in his late teens, he spent his career in the corporate world, holding senior positions in a number of countries across the African continent.

In 2017 he and his wife, Belinda, immigrated to Canada, settling in Vancouver. In 2020 they moved to Nova Scotia, purchasing an inn in the picturesque Digby area.

Greg has always enjoyed a passion for fiction, and has always harboured an ambition to join those who have added their own contribution to this wonderful art.